Louis Schnabel

Voegele's Marriage and Other Tales

Louis Schnabel

Voegele's Marriage and Other Tales

ISBN/EAN: 9783337343927

Printed in Europe, USA, Canada, Australia, Japan

Cover: Foto ©Andreas Hilbeck / pixelio.de

More available books at **www.hansebooks.com**

SPECIAL SERIES. No. 2.

VOEGELE'S MARRIAGE

AND

OTHER TALES

BY

LOUIS SCHNABEL.

ISRAEL'S MISSION IS PEACE

Philadelphia:

THE JEWISH PUBLICATION SOCIETY OF AMERICA.

1892.

To JOSEPH WEISSE,
>   *Rabbi in Waag-Neustadt, Hungary:*

Several years ago a Jewish author published a book, which he dedicated "AU BON DIEU." Mindful of Rabbi Elazar ben Shamua's saying: "Let the fear of thy master be as thy fear of God," I partly follow the example set by this Frenchman, and take the liberty, my revered teacher, of placing your name at the head of this little volume.

In most of the sketches, the actors date from a time when I was very young, a pupil in the school where you were master, and a little later on, when already a youth, but still enjoying the privilege of your guiding hand in my studies, and the added happiness of being counted a member of your household, at the period when you were installed as rabbi and began your career.

Since then, to be sure, forty-five Springs have passed over my head, but youth is the poetry that accompanies us through life like an invisible perfume, and I still love to think of, and in spirit transplant myself to the old school-room and the family circle so dear to me, and again, as then, admire your untiring diligence, your scholarship, your elegant Hebrew style, but above all your pious, patriarchal life.

The beneficial influence you exercised on me in my early days has never left me on my pilgrimage through life, and will vanish only with my last breath.

To you, my revered teacher, I owe my love to God, to my religion, my race and all mankind.

Accept this homage as a small sign of my gratitude and an expression of the high respect with which I sign myself,
Your humble and obedient servant,
LOUIS SCHNABEL.

CONTENTS.

VOEGELE'S MARRIAGE.

"And were I to try five hundred times more to commit to memory this long-winded, never-ending second commandment, I am quite sure I should no more be able to recite it by heart, word for word, than if I had never looked into my catechism," exclaimed Voegele, angrily, striking her little fist against her forehead. "I shall never succeed in finding my way among all the likenesses and graven images and other gods in which it abounds, without getting 'out' somewhere in the midst of my recitation, either in the 'heaven above' or on the 'earth beneath,' or in the 'waters under the earth.'"

"And how will you fare at the examination?" asked her sister Miriam, who, though only two years older, was the happy mother of four children.

"I am sure I don't know myself. But what can I do? As long as Mayor Bartosh insists on a literal recitation of the ten commandments and of the other paragraphs in their immediate neighborhood, I shall not be able to pass my examination, and consequently not obtain my marriage license, unless God, in His mercy, makes another person, in some miraculous way, recite for me, while I keep silent. Voegele, Voegele!" she added, shaking her curly head, "why have you not sister Miriam's clever head on your shoulders? You would to-day no longer be called Voegele Loeb, but Frau Kurtz."

For a better understanding of Voegele's dread of the examination that awaited her, and for a more intimate acquaintance with her and Miriam, it will be necessary to sketch for my readers a short biography of the two sisters. Born of indigent parents in a small town in Moravia, Austria, the two girls went to the congregational school, there to acquire the three R's, at the same time taking at home private lessons in Hebrew reading. After leaving school, they started a small business, selling ribbons and knick-knacks, at first in the market-place of their town; and having succeeded in their native place, they soon carried their wares to neighboring towns. By thrift and perseverance, they so largely increased the number of their customers that, after some years, they were able to open a shop and raise their firm to a certain respectability.

The sisters resembled each other so much that very often they were taken one for another. Miriam, the elder of the two, gained the heart of a well-to-do young merchant, who admired her practical business methods and her man-like independence, combined with a full dose of common-sense. There was but one obstacle in the way of their becoming man and wife, and that was the cruel matrimonial laws governing the country at the time when these events took place.

The principle underlying these inhuman laws, exceptionally made against the Jews in Moravia, was the same which, 3,385 years ago, gave rise to the famous Pharaonic decree: "Every son that is born ye shall cast into the river." Like the King of Egypt, the Austrian government said: "Come, let us deal wisely with them, lest they multiply and wax exceeding mighty." After the census of the Jews in Moravia had been taken, the government promulgated these new marriage laws, ordaining that the given number of the heads of families in any congregation should from that day not be increased but remain stationary. When diminished by death, any first-born was, under certain conditions, entitled to apply for a marriage license to fill the vacancy. The second-born had such a privilege only when there was no first-born candidate. It need not be mentioned that the natural longevity of our people excluded the third-born entirely.

Any application for obtaining a marriage certificate had to be supplemented by half-a-dozen or more certificates written on stamped paper, showing: (1) That P. T. had died. (2) That the applicant was born in no other congregation than his. (3) That his name was entered in the register of births. (4) That he was vaccinated. (5) That he had attended the parochial school. (6) That his moral standing was unexceptional. (7) That he had the means of supporting a family.

Equipped with these documents, the applicant had to climb the steps of the government ladder, beginning at the lowest round, at the Mayor's office, up to that of the Secretary of the Interior Department, and at each step some government officer had to be bribed merely for obtaining the promise that his application-papers would not be stored away to slumber in some pigeon-hole, under a thick layer of dust, till the applicant himself returned to dust.

When, at last, the marriage license was granted, sealed with the large government seal, and addressed without the conventional " Herrn," but simply and offensively " To the Jew P. T. in P.," there remained but one more difficulty to be surmounted. The groom and his bride both had to undergo an examination showing their proficiency in catechism, and so deep-felt was the paternal

love of the government toward its Jewish subjects and
its tender care for the maintenance of their religion,
that the law made the Christian mayors examiners in
preference to the rabbis, for fear that the rabbis might
be too lenient toward the members of their flocks.

Some of these Austrian bureaucrats were exceptionally pedantic and punctilious, like Mayor Bartosh, Voegele's *bête noire*, but the great majority were rather
inclined to indulgence, particularly when the candidate
introduced himself with an envelope in hand containing
some sort of a *douceur*.

David Russ, Miriam's intended, was a third-born,
consequently a hopeless case. When celebrating the
first anniversary of their betrothal, Miriam said to her
intended, in a business-like way: " David, my love, why
should we wait any longer, and let the Spring of our
life pass away? Do you wish to wait till the Messiah
comes and then be married in the Holy Land?"   And,
practical as Miriam was, she did not even leave him
time enough to ponder much the importance of this
step.

One day, running home from school to my dinner,
while passing before David Russ' house, I noticed that
all the blinds were closed, and it seemed to me as if a
gleam of candle-light pierced through the two round
holes of the shutters. I stopped a moment before the
door to guess at what was going on inside.

" Come in, dear boy; you can help us to perform a
mitzvah" (holy commandment), said an elderly man to
me, as he suddenly appeared at the door ; " you are the
tenth person wanted for our *minian*" (the number of
male persons required for a prayer-meeting), and, without waiting for my consent, he ushered me into the

room. On my arrival the whole company, who seemed
to have waited for me, left the room, and taking the
candles from the table, we climbed up a ladder leading
to the garret.

The expression *garret-marriage*, so often used in the
Judengasse, had always puzzled me. I could never
comprehend its deeper meaning. Now I was to learn
its signification by having it plainly exhibited before
my eyes. In place of the *huppah* (canopy), a *tallith*
(white cloth with tassels on the four corners, worn by
males during the act of offering prayers), was spread
out and held out by four young men over the heads of
the couple, in front of whom the elderly man officiated
instead of a rabbi. While whispering the benedictions
he looked anxiously about in every nook and corner of
the garret, as if fearing he might discover somewhere a
policeman in citizen's clothes. When reading the
khetubah (marriage-contract), he swallowed the words
in haste, as if they burned his tongue; even the little
assembly seemed nervous and impatient to leave
the forbidden ground. Crying, laughing, amen, every
sign of participation in the singular ceremony came
forth in suppressed tones—a whispering all around.
The glass was hardly trod upon and broken, and the
masol tob (good luck) exchanged, when half of the
company was already on the steps of the ladder, descend-
ing quickly, as if they were leaving Egypt pursued by
a detachment of Egyptian horsemen. The whole affair
looked more like a funeral than a marriage ceremony.

History repeats itself. So had Gideon to beat out his
wheat in the wine-press, instead of on the threshing-floor,
to hide it from the Midianites.

The danger to which the officiating old man, together

with the married couple and the bystanders, had exposed themselves, was, indeed, very great; for had an Austrian detective peeped through a crack of the roof and discovered our proceedings, we would have been surely sent to the State Prison for a long period, ranging variously from five to twenty years. Fortunately, there was no law forbidding a girl to wear a cap, and so Miriam could on the following day appear in the street, her head ornamented with a white lace cap, the distinguishing mark of a married woman, and be recognized as such by old and young of her own people.

When I told my mother what I had just witnessed, she could not find words enough to praise me for having taken a share in such a God-pleasing work, for which God would surely reward me at some future day.

"Your share," she said, "is the dividend of a capital that will bear high interest, which you will enjoy in this world, while the capital will be reserved for you in the world to come."

To give me a foretaste of the interest that I was going to enjoy in this world, my mother picked out for me from the basket the choicest apple she could find, and kissing me before my return to school she said: "I hope I shall live to see you, my dear son, conducted to the *huppah*."

Not so fortunate was Voegele. Ten years had already passed since the day she was betrothed to Herman Kurtz. Herman, a second-born, had competed for a number of years against his equals as well as against first-born candidates. To record the history of his troubles in obtaining his marriage license would require more space than the size of the frame which I have selected for my story would allow. You could have

listened to him for hours when he narrated all the efforts
he had to make, merely for obtaining access to the different government offices, and when he unfolded before
his friends the picture of all the humiliations he had to
endure. In commemoration of those days of misery, he
kept in his safe an old worn hat of doubtful color and
indefinite shape, a relic which he used to exhibit on such
occasions as a mute witness of his former disappoint-.
ments. At the sight of this crushed hat, the hours spent
in ante-chambers with janitors, footmen, clerks and other
creatures, rose vividly in his mind. He remembered
how often this vile hat had been in his hands instead of
on his head.

"And, after all, what was it that I strove for?" he
used to say. "Was it for an office, or any gift or favor?
No, I only asked not to be deprived of my innate,
natural rights. But in order to obtain these inalienable
rights, I had to sacrifice self-respect, honor, time and
money, laboring for those rights at all seasons of the
year, in cold, in wind, in rain and mud, always on the
go, knocking at doors, and always, no! and no! again
and again!"

When his story reached its climax and Herman grew
hotly excited at the simple recitation of his by-gone
troubles, he used to cast this hat on the floor and to
trample upon it as if to avenge former sufferings.

After ten years of unrelenting cares and struggles, he
obtained, at last, the right, or, as expressed in government style, the "concession" to marry and be happy.
The sheet of paper on which this concession was written,
was a precious document, indeed, for the amount of
money it cost him could have bought him a valuable
piece of property; and as the little bags of coin, which

formerly occupied his safe, had changed quarters, and moved into the government coffers, he had now plenty of room for accommodating therein both his crumpled hat and his crumpled rights.

The party of the first part (excuse the legal phraseology) was now ready for the marriage contract, but how about the party of the second part? Poor Voegele did her best to memorize the second commandment, but it was to her a bitter pill which she could not swallow. The more she studied it the larger its dimensions seemed to grow, and she wished Mayor Bartosh were either in the "heaven above" or, at least, "under the earth." When at last that awful examination day had come, and with it Bartosh and his favorite second commandment, Voegele recited it quite well at the beginning, making her way without the least accident through "heaven, earth and water," but when near the end she got confused at the "jealous God" and entangled in "the third and fourth generation," and, as she had to stop reciting, she began to cry.

"Voegele," said Mayor Bartosh, "though I feel very sorry for you, I am bound to postpone your marriage. There can be no happiness in conjugal life without the ten commandments, and the second one is not the least important. Prepare yourself for another examination. In three months you may be able to pass it creditably."

Voegele dared not expose herself to a second mortification, for she was quite sure she should never master the second commandment, and she felt that some miracle would have to be wrought for her sake,

To push matters ahead, Miriam, the energetic little woman, tried her powers at performing such a miracle. "Did not Jacob, the younger brother, obtain his father

Isaac's blessing by disguising himself and personating his brother Esau, and why could not I, the elder sister, personate Voegele and so accomplish the ends we have in view?"

No sooner said than done. Taking off her lace cap, and arranging her hair in Voegele's style, she took her sister to the looking-glass, and putting her arm around her waist, said to her: "Pray, tell me now, which is Voegele and which is Miriam?" And that intrepid little woman hastened away to the mayor's office, submitted to the examination, and took both the mayor and the second commandment by storm.

"That tyrant of a mayor," said Miriam, when she reported to her family the success of her exploit, "stood before me as stiff and immovable as if he were himself a 'graven image' of the nether world, and measured me with his piercing glance from head to toe, but I was not in the least afraid of my second commandment-man. My heaviest piece of artillery I had well posted for the attack of 'any other gods' from whatever region they might come, and in a very short time he and his auxiliary troops were utterly routed and in full retreat.

"'Voegele,' said he to me, as I started to go, 'you have passed an excellent examination. By Moses and the prophets! you have done exceedingly well.' Then he pinched my cheek and whispered in my ear some such complimentary words, that I had to collect all my thoughts not to betray my *rôle*, by telling him that my eldest son had already passed his tenth year.

"'In the course of this week,' he called after me when going down the stairs, 'I will send you your marriage license.'"

The lucky turn things had taken, and the manner

with which Miriam had brought them about was a
matter of congratulation to all concerned in the happiness of our couple. But a secret, once revealed, will
soon find its way where it is least expected. Some of
Herman's disappointed competitors may have, in a moment of jealousy, contributed their share toward carrying it into the mayor's office.

"I must examine Voegele once more," cried Jupiter
Bartosh, with a voice of thunder, to David Russ, who
had come to answer the summons sent to Voegele to
appear before the mayor, and to excuse her absence on
account of her illness, "she must be re-examined. No
marriage without second commandment."

However, in spite of little Jupiter's threats, Voegele
was lawfully and publicly married to her Herman, even
without the tyrant's consent.

This event came to pass in a miraculous way, as she
always used to predict it would, in her moments of despair at her bad memory. The Messiah seemed to have
come for her sake.

Prince Metternich, the powerful minister of state, who
for nearly forty years had exercised, almost without con-
trol, the highest authority in the Austrian Empire, was
compelled to take flight from Vienna before Voegele
Loeb could become Frau Kurtz.

Forsooth, Israel's Redeemer, had once more stretched
out his mighty arm, and in old-fashioned, old-testament-
like way, sent his Messiah to liberate his people from the
hand of their oppressors. This Messiah was the great
revolution of 1848.

Toward the end of February of that year, a rumor
spread from the mayor's office that a revolution had
broken out in Paris, that the French had turned out

their citizen king, Louis Philippe, set fire in the open street to the royal throne, and proclaimed a republican government.

On the twelfth of March, a revolution broke out in Vienna, and two days thereafter, liberty, equality and fraternity were proclaimed throughout the whole empire. Among the first victims to the cause of liberty were a number of Jewish students, who were laid with Christian companions in arms in the same grave, and it seemed as if every prejudice and religious hatred were from that moment banished from the land forever.

A new era began. "The snares of wickedness were opened, undone the bands of the yoke, and the oppressed let free." The trembling structure of oppressive exceptional laws crumbled to pieces, and the Jews all over the empire began to inhale the sweet air of liberty.

"I am sorry," Herman used to say in those happy days, "that I was not present at the burning of the royal throne in Paris. I should have liked to throw into the flames my marriage license, which, though it cost me a royal fortune, is of no earthly use to me now. It would have been a satisfaction to me to offer both the government's 'concession' and the crumpled hat as burnt-offerings to atone for my past humiliations and struggles; they would at least have perished in decent company."

Herman and Voegele were the first couple that were allowed to come before the rabbi and ask him to make them man and wife without being obliged to produce their marriage license.

After having addressed to them a few words of exhortation about their future conjugal life, the rabbi said to Herman: "With your permission I should like to solemnize your wedding ceremony, it being the first in

this new era of our political life, by performing it on a
larger scale. Let me explain. You know, Mr. Kurtz,
that there are in our congregation fifty-nine heads of
families whom the civil laws consider as single men and
whose offspring are entered in the register of births as
illegitimate children, who are not even allowed to be
called by the names of their fathers. According to the
'laws of Moses and Israel' they are, to all intents and
purposes, lawfully married, and their children as legitimate as my own. There will be really no necessity for my
renewing the marriage bonds by which they are united.
However, in my twofold capacity as religious teacher
and civil officer, it lies in my power to restore to them
the rights of which former oppressive laws have deprived
them, by publicly reconstructing their union. Thus
reconstructed, they, their wives and children will be
the equals of their fellow-citizens, and I can then blot
out from the civil register the disgrace and contumely
which years of persecution and intolerance have heaped
upon them."

The fifty-nine couples our good rabbi spoke about, like
David and Miriam, had had their marriages clandes-
tinely performed in a garret, and these garret-marriages
were now to be proclaimed legitimate.

Herman and Voegele's wedding ceremony was indeed
the most impressive ever witnessed in any synagogue or
church. With them came the fifty-nine other couples
accompanied by their offspring, consisting of no less
than three hundred sons and daughters, to share with
them the blessing of the rabbi.

When the rabbi had finished his most eloquent ser-
mon, and mutual congratulations had been exchanged,
Frau Rosie Spitz, accompanied by her six children,

approached the rabbi, and said to him, while offering him her snuff-box, which she drew out of the pocket of her bridal dress, " Dear Rabbi, allow me to introduce to you my daughter Leah. She is engaged to be married, and we expect that her wedding will take place next month."

In leaving the synagogue, Miriam, clinging to David's side, said to her sister, " Voegele dear, take Herman's arm. In such a crowd, and among so many newly married couples, I shouldn't wonder if some old bridegroom would take you home, exchanging, by mistake, his old wife for a young one," and turning to her husband she added, archly : " Your ' other gods ' of the second commandment are not by far so terrible as ' other men.' "

GRANDMOTHER'S VOW.

The persons acting in this story lay but yesterday buried under the rubbish of past years; to-day they rise, striving to come to the surface and return to life again.

I am a child again, and I feel the sensation of hearing grandmother's brown silk Sabbath-dress rustle. She opens the door, and I run to meet her, in order that she may lay her hands upon my head and bless me.

"A good Sabbath to you, dear grandmother!" But instead of returning my salutation, she only looks at me, her face beaming with joy, and, while passing her bony fingers over my cheek, she discloses to my eyes her prayer-book, which darts beams of gladness into my heart.

The lovely prayer-book—does it not contain a real treasure for me, a tid-bit, which I would not exchange for the most precious stone? To be sure, in the course of time the book has lost its former youthful freshness, and the leaves, turned yellow, are now wrinkled, like grandmother's face, but the length of years could no more detract from its sanctity than they could impair its owner's loveliness.

This prayer-book, which the old lady used to carry on her way to the synagogue, was wrapped in a white lace handkerchief, as the Levites in ancient times carried the ark of the testimony, veiled all over, so that no stranger might see the holy object. Besides the book and the old lady's eye-glasses, the white wrapper inclosed a ginger-cake, quite as long as the book, though not as thick, of a shining dark-brown color, and having an almond set in the centre.

Though more than half a century has passed since I enjoyed the last ginger-cake dear grandmother brought me with her Sabbath blessing, I still remember every little circumstance connected with her Sabbath morning visits. I have not even forgotten how delighted I used to be with my tid-bit, and how I attacked it, first at the four corners, changing the square at each bite to a circle and reserving for my last bite the from heaven-fallen, manna-like almond.

After me it was my mother's turn to bow her head before her mother. While these two thus faced each other as for an embrace, one gave and the other received the blessing.

"Your Sabbath-cap is again awry, dear mother," was my mother's invariable remark every Sabbath when that ceremony was over. "Please sit down a minute and let me arrange it for you." And the old lady, while willingly submitting to that operation, would smilingly reply in a set formula of excuse: "Dear, foolish baby, who cares? Don't you know that I have made a vow never to use a looking-glass?"

At the crier's call, "To the synagogue!" sounding from the street, we hastened away so as not to arrive late.

Thus it was ever the same, year in and year out. Summer, winter, rain or sunshine, never brought about the least change. Grandmother ever wore the same rustling, brown silk dress, brought me the same kind of ginger-cake, blessed me, then my mother, who never forgot to notice the oblique position of the old lady's

cap; nor did grandmother ever change the least word
in her formula: "Dear, foolish baby, who cares?
Don't you know that I have made a vow never to use
a looking-glass?"

It was but natural in a child that this mysterious
vow roused my curiosity as to the reason why grandmother denied herself the innocent pleasure of seeing
her stately figure in a looking-glass while putting on
her Sabbath-cap, and I would have gladly relinquished
my much-desired cake, yea, even the almond, in
exchange for this looking-glass mystery, had either of
the ladies been willing to disclose it to me.

"Is there any law in the Bible forbidding one to look
into a mirror on the Sabbath-day?" I once asked her,
on our way to the synagogue.

"Foolish little boy, you ought to know that better
than I, since you have learned the whole Pentateuch,
from 'In the beginning,' to 'In the sight of all Israel,'"
she answered, sneeringly.

"I am pretty sure that there is not the least reference
to a mirror to be found in the Pentateuch. I, therefore,
cannot understand why my grandmother need be stricter
than strict," I ventured to remark like a little professor
ex cathedrâ.

"Be still!" she interposed, somewhat harshly. "Such
a little boy, and were he ever so clever, must not know
everything."

Years rolled on. The little boy became a young
man. The brown silk dress rustled no more. Since
many a Sabbath it hung lonely and forgotten, in a corner of the wardrobe, on the same hook with the cap.
The ginger-cake was a thing of the past, and, when I
wished to receive grandmother's blessing, I had to bow

down over the old lady's sick-bed, and to lift her languid hands over my head. Her prayer-book and eyeglasses lay, without their white wrapper, uncovered, upon a little table beside her bed, without their third companion. In former years, these three objects had been so inseparably connected in my mind with the Sabbath, nay, so entirely interwoven with it, that now, when I saw them every day on that little table, it seemed to me as if the Sabbath-day had lost part of its sanctity.

In her old age, poor grandmother had become an invalid, and, in her helpless condition, I had the satisfaction of requiting all the kindness she had shown me in my boyhood.

Her former stately figure was now reduced to such an extent that I could carry her in my arms like a baby; and this office I performed every day when her bed had to be made—a performance which she thought no one in the house could succeed in better than I.

In an exceptionally talkative mood, grandmother said to me, one morning: "Laser, my dear, last night while I lay awake, I tried to pass my time in counting up the number of ginger-cakes I should have brought you, were I yet able to step into your mother's house on my way to the synagogue, but my head has become so weak that I could not make it out. How many cakes do I owe you up to date?" she said, smilingly.

"A little grandmother must not know everything, and were she ever so adorable," I replied, imitating the gestures with which she had uttered her refusal when she cut short my question, on our way to the synagogue. "Never mind the number. I know they might fill a goodly-sized packing-box, but I am willing to give up

every claim in exchange for the answer which you once
refused to the foolish little boy."

There was no short-hand writer present while grandmother told me that long-expected story, but I shall try
to make the best of it.

*   *   *   *   *   *   *   *   *

At the age of sixteen, my grandmother was not only
a handsome, stylish girl, but also well-educated, though
not possessing our modern acquirements of culture and
refinement. Piano playing, foreign languages, elocu-
tion, drawing, dancing, and similar accomplishments
were considered in her time, and in her social circumstances and surroundings, as special studies for artists.
But instead of all these, she was admired for her melo-
dious voice when chanting either the morning or evening prayers in the Hebrew language, be it observed,
word for word from memory, without the omission of a
word or the mumbling of the least syllable, but just as
if she were a professional synagogue-reader. She was,
moreover, an accomplished housekeeper and cook, and
her kitchen and scullery looked, at all times of the day,
as clean and neat as the best-kept apothecary shop.

No wonder, then, that young Laser Broch, only two
years her senior, fell in love with her, and took her
home as his bride.

A week after their wedding, Laser, starting on a business journey to Vienna, took his young wife along, in
order to show her the imperial capital. The young
woman had never crossed the boundaries of her
native place, and the town-hall, the church, and synagogue, all of them out of repair, she considered master-
works of architectural art.

You may imagine how overpowering must have been

the impression the imperial city made on her. The noise and bustle of the multitude crowding the sidewalk, and the rattling of the carriages on the stone pavement, kept her nerves in continuous excitement.

"You might live as long as Methuselah, and have a thousand eyes instead of two, and yet be but poorly equipped for being everywhere and looking at everything in this great city," she said to her husband.

Laser, having been previously in Vienna, was less amused by the sights he saw than by the rural innocence which his beloved wife exhibited on every occasion of first beholding anything new to her limited experience.

Exuberant with youthful gaiety, he teased her to his heart's content, and had chance offered him some practical joke, he would not have shrunk from playing it on her.

One day, he took her to a coffee-house which was situated in one of the most fashionable quarters of the city. It had been opened only a month previously, was beautifully painted, furnished in French style, with chairs and sofas covered with garnet plush. Between every two windows were gilt-framed looking-glasses, extending from the ceiling down to white marble tables, on which they seemed to rest.

The rows of looking-glasses through which she had to pass, dazzling her at first, soon invited the young daughter of Eve to behold in them her slender figure, which she examined from different points of view at every step she made forward. Nor was she at a loss for the choice of a table. She quite naturally selected one between two windows, and seated herself facing the looking-glass, her back turned toward the main entrance. Being so near her own reflection that she could almost kiss herself, she could not resist the temptation of being entirely absorbed by that radiant image.

Soon a *marqueur* (so they call a waiter in Vienna) stood by their table, and with a graceful bow asked for orders. He was attired in a black, swallow-tail coat, white cravat, and low-cut patent-leather shoes. Presently, he served the breakfast on a tray, which nearly covered the whole table.

At a glance, the young woman noticed a number of things which seemed to her quite superfluous for a breakfast of coffee and bread. She wondered who ordered him to bring two bottles filled to the brim with ice water. Then she looked at the big coffee-pot and the milk pitchers, and the various little plates, and saucers, and spoons, which to her mind might have been an ample set for a family of five. Moreover, two napkins, ironed as smoothly as a pair of cuffs and artistically folded, were to be used just for one meal, and then be thrown in the wash. "Oh, dear," she thought, "such extravagance might break one's heart. Heavens, what luxury!" In her parents' house she had never witnessed such splendor; never, not even at her own wedding feast.

What puzzled her above all things were the elegant suit of the *marqueur* and his noble and gentlemanly bearing. Only a great personage, such as the mayor, the highest civil authority in the town, had she seen in such attire, and only on Corpus Christi day, when marching in a procession to the church.

"Two bottles of water! What in the world is all this water for? Who would pour water into an empty stomach, or who would drink cold water with warm coffee? Is not coffee itself a most appropriate beverage for quenching one's thirst? Did my mother, did I ever dream of setting a pitcher of water on a breakfast table?"

Such were the reflections young Frau Broch made while enjoying her cup of the world-renowned Vienna coffee. After pondering for some time, she thought she at last found the solution to her various puzzles. One enigma gave her the clue to the other. These two bottles of water seemed to her the natural explanation of the *marqueur's* exquisite black suit.

To be quite sure of being on the right path, she wished first to sound her husband, in order to see whether he would substantiate her conjectures, and she managed it in a way which would have done honor to an old diplomat.

"Laser, my love," she said, "I don't see any women in this building. I wonder who washes these numerous plates, cups and saucers?"

"Do I understand you to ask me who are the dish-washers of this place?" he answered.

"Certainly," she said, "you don't believe that such a good-looking, well-dressed gentleman would submit to the degradation of washing dishes, do you?"

At that moment, a teasing little Puck passed rapidly through his head, and deposited there the thought of a trick, which Laser determined to play on his innocent little wife.

"Who does the dish-washing here?" he repeated, with a most serious mien. "Who else but the guests themselves. Why, this man looks not less venerable than the president of our congregation. Has he not prepared for you everything you require? Two bottles filled with water and two napkins? Do you wish for anything else? To be sure, he could not have made it more comfortable for you, could he?"

The young woman felt now like a fish in the water.

Tucking up her sleeves and pinning a napkin as an apron around her waist, she feasted once more upon her lovely, reflected figure. She had never washed her dishes at home in such elegant surroundings. This comparison naturally reminded her vividly of father, mother, brothers and sisters, so that during this general cleaning up she entirely forgot that she was facing the large mirror.

The young bride showed herself quite an artist, and was not a little proud when she noticed that her husband had not turned his eyes from her, while he admired her handiness.

She was now at the last bowl containing the collective dish-water, and while considering how to dispose of it, a gentleman went out of the room and left the door ajar. At the same moment she chanced to glance at the looking-glass, and was agreeably surprised to notice the *mirrored* half-opened door, allowing a view into the street. This moment was most opportune for throwing the dish-water into the street. Rapidly she lifted her hand on high, and in an instant the brownish fluid was discharged—oh, dear—not into the street, but on the looking-glass, splashing at the same time her brown silk dress and her husband's coat.

Imagine the consternation and indignation with which she left the coffee-house.

But while Laser laughed heartily on their way to the hotel, she vowed, tempestuously: "May I lose the sight of both my eyes, if I ever look at myself again in a looking-glass!"

We know already how faithfully she kept her vow.

In the good old times such a vow was not by any means as terrible as it might seem in our days, for on week-days our house-wives had really no time to stand before the looking-glass, and they did not even care so much for it, because on their wedding-day they had to part with their braids or curls. Before the bride's head was covered and attired for the procession to the marriage ceremony, a pair of inexorable scissors made terrible havoc of the most luxuriant hair.

This event of the coffee-house did not in the least disturb the happy conjugal life of my grandparents. In grandfather's lifetime, grandmother Sarah wore her Sabbath-cap as neatly as could be desired, because grandfather used to perform the service of a waiting-woman, and as often as she started for the synagogue on a Sabbath morning, he would step in her way, and, while she embraced him, he arranged her cap, as she remarked to him:

"Laser, my love, there is a little side-door to every vow by which you may evade it, and so it is in my case. I shall certainly keep mine truly and faithfully. But could any one forbid me to see my picture in your beloved eyes?"

A MYSTIFIED ANGEL.

Have you ever noticed on a green tree a dried branch which, in spite of rains and storms, clings to the parent trunk as if it could forever resist time and decay? Its leaves are dried and parched, and its moisture has been absorbed by scorching sunbeams. Its hold on the tree is limited to but a very thin strip of bark, through which the roots send scanty nourishment in order to preserve the last functions of life in an otherwise dead branch. This connection, though so weak and frail that it could be severed without effort by a child's hand, is often very tenacious when left to itself. Yea, heavy wind-gusts assailing and shaking the tree with raging fury, seemingly uprooting the trunk itself, do not harm this thin bark-strip in the least, while other branches full of sap and vitality break down and are felled to the ground.

Grandmother Sarah was the picture of such a dried branch on the tree of life.

During the last ten years of her life, which in her suffering seemed to last an eternity, she had no more ardent desire, no more fervent longing than to obtain the grace of changing this valley of tears for the realm of eternity.

As a wanderer through the desert " panteth after brooks of water," so the blind, paralyzed matron longed for the hour of release.

Poor grandmother! During ten years she recited her *Adon Olam* with so much devotion, particularly that last verse: "In thy hand I trust my spirit, whether I am asleep or awake, and with my spirit my body. The

Lord is with me and I fear not." This beautiful hymn she sang with so much earnestness that one could hear it was not to her an "acquired precept of man," but the true expression of her innermost feelings, and she even added in her own words the prayer that the Almighty might call her unto him during the night.

Strange to say, as soon as after a sleepless night the first morning rays brought the daylight into her room, the morning *Sh'ma* was on her lips, and she thanked the "Creator of light" for it, although it had brought no change to the blind woman. And, in contradiction to her night-prayer, she thanked God for "the life granted her," and for "the soul returned to her," and asked that "He might preserve her in the future."

Surely the angel of prayer, who has the mission to carry the morning and evening prayers of mortals before the throne of the Immortal, must have found it impossible to perform his task in this special case. To harmonize grandmother's morning wishes with her nightly prayers must have been trying even to the patience of an angel, and since he could not reconcile them the mystified angel did not forward them at all, and thus her prayers remained unanswered.

Grandmother Sarah neither lived nor died.

At last the Omniscient had mercy on her and granted her salvation.

One Friday evening, when the Sabbath lamp was lit, my father coming home from the synagogue intoned the old Hebrew hymn, to welcome the Sabbath angels, who on the Sabbath eve bring rest and happiness to every Jewish house that is festively decorated in honor of the holy day. His numerous family joined in the refrain: "Peace with ye, ye angels of peace, angels of the Most High, sent by the King of kings, **the Holy,** blessed be He."

Among the Sabbath angels there must have stolen in another angel who had a different mission to perform. This angel stayed not with the company around the table, which was covered with a shining white cloth, nor did he seem to bring to the festively attired family that quiet and blessing which an honest Sabbath angel imprints on the forehead of every Jewish child as a reflection of God's rest. He could not have stayed in the lit room, but must have instantly gone to the dim alcove, and placed himself at the head of grandmother's sickbed.

When the last sounds of the hymn had died away, the whole family went to the alcove. One after the other bowed down and lifted the paralyzed hand of the old lady upon his head to receive her blessing.

Grandmother must have felt a presentiment of the coming of her welcome guest.

"Laser," she said to her favorite grandchild, who bore the name of her husband, "after supper you will bring me the psalms, some of which you will read to me. I must prepare to-night some provision for my long journey, for I feel that the Lord, blessed be His name, has found me worthy of calling me to Him for eternal rest, on this holy Sabbath, as a recompense for my many sufferings, and for my resignation to His holy will."

Accustomed since many years to similar expressions, her family took no notice of them but went to their supper.

When father had closed the "sanctification" of the Sabbath with the benediction, "Blessed art Thou, Eternal, who sanctified the Sabbath," a sonorous

"Amen" was heard, coming from the alcove, and immediately after: "Hear, O Israel, the Eternal, our God, the Eternal is One," so full-sounding that we suspected some other person must be in the sick-room. All of us rose horror-stricken from our seats, and hastened to the sick-bed.

The old lady who for years had been unable to move her limbs, sat upright, as if supported by an invisible hand, her face turned toward the head of her bed, her shrunken eyelids wide open as if to regain her sight once more, and her arm horizontally stretched out.

"Wait, Laser, wait; dear husband, I am coming, I am coming!" she cried, and fell back on her pillow.

The Angel of Death had performed his mission. Grandmother Sarah was no more.

THE STORY OF AN EPITAPH.

I.

On a beautiful May morning of the year 1854, I stood in the cemetery of P., in front of a six-feet-high tombstone, and copied into my note-book the inscription engraved in Hebrew letters.

Thanks to the willow with its rich foliage and numerous branches hanging down to the stone's base, thus protecting it from dust and rain, the black characters of the epitaph and the gilt letters of the acrostic were as fresh and shining as if the engraver had finished them but a few hours ago.

At the head you could clearly read:

> Here lies
> the virgin *Perl*, daughter of Solomon *Sanger*,
> Death snatched her away in the twenty-first
> year of her life.
> Born, Tishri 18th, 5591.
> Died, Kislev 15th, 5611.

Then followed twelve lines of the epitaph, so poetically and so intellectually written that it bore a striking resemblance to the sublime language of the prophets, and I thought it worthy of the pen of the great poet Jehudah Hallevi.

I was just going to put my note-book and pencil into my side-pocket, when I felt my shoulder gently touched. In the first moment of surprise, while turning around, the note-book and pencil dropped from my hand.

" Pardon, sir," said the stranger, as he moved toward the tombstone, seated himself on the base, and leaned his head on the edge of the stone, spreading his feet as if sitting in an arm-chair, " may I ask you whether you communicate with the world of spirits ?"

The person addressing me, a strikingly handsome man, completely dressed in mourning, sat before me, a picture of grief.

Without turning my eyes from him, I answered, " Sir, I do not believe in spiritualism, nor will I ever become a spiritualist ; neither have I any desire whatever to be in communication with the dead."

" What else are you looking for here, in the solitude of the cemetery, on this grave ?" he asked, while scrutinizing me.

" I am collecting well-written epitaphs," I replied, " which I intend to compile and publish."

"A singular idea. But that among all the tombstones just this one should have attracted you, and kept you so long on this spot, makes me suspect that something more than mere fondness for tombstone inscriptions must have brought you hither. It seems to me almost," he whispered, in mysterious, awful sounds which made me shiver, "as if you were, like me, acquainted with the mystery, or rather history, of this epitaph."

" I pledge you my word of honor," I replied, " that your suspicion is entirely without foundation, and that it was nothing but the elegant style of the poem that attracted me so much. Besides," I added, " I have been in P. for a few hours only, and have neither known the deceased nor even heard of her before."

" Do not misconstrue my words," the stranger interrupted. " I did not speak at all of the history of the girl; I mentioned expressly the history of the *epitaph.*"

He closed his speech abruptly, cast one more scrutinizing glance at me, rose from his seat and gazed a few moments at the gilt-lettered name—Perl Sanger. Tears glided down his cheeks and passed away in his beard. He then turned quickly about, and left the grave with its tombstone.

"We shall meet again!" he called to me, and disappeared as mysteriously as he came. I wished to inquire for his name and address, but it was too late; he was already out of sight.

Now I prepared to leave the "good place," as the German Jews call the burial-ground; and stooping down on the grassy mound in order to pick up my note-book and pencil, I found in the grass a black-edged visiting card, bearing the inscription :

DR. JULIUS LEVIN.

II.

The Café de l'Exposition, on the Boulevard des Capucines, was patronized during the first Parisian Industrial Exposition mostly by Englishmen. Of Frenchmen, especially Parisians, but few were to be met there, and those were only elderly, gray-haired people. Neither billiards nor dominos nor any other game that might disturb the quiet-loving readers of the daily papers were allowed to be played in this locality. The place looked more like an aristocratic English parlor than like a *café*. Being a passionate reader of papers myself, I patronized that locality and soon belonged to its regular frequenters.

One day I read in the *Revue des Deux Mondes* an essay on magnetism, of which the following passage attracted my attention

* * * So great is the magnetic power of man's eyes that they can force a person to interrupt himself, be he ever so much absorbed in reading the most interesting book. This interruption may be brought about by looking steadfastly at a person, who soon begins to feel the magnetic attraction of the fixed eyes, and involuntarily directs his glance toward the one by whom he is influenced.

This passage struck me. Was it the desire to convince myself of the truth of this statement, or was it my childish curiosity to see how I should succeed in making the experiment? I cannot tell now what led me to do it. Closing the pamphlet, I leaned my head against the red velvet cushion of my arm-chair and stared persistently at a gentleman who seemed to be absorbed in reading the *Cologne Gazette*.

I had scarcely looked at him a minute when he suddenly lifted his head and directed his eyes towards me. In order to avert any suspicion of my action, I now closed my eyes, simulating sleep, and remained a few minutes in this position. To tell the truth, I dared no more look at my *vis-à-vis*, because I suspected that it was now his turn to gaze at me, and because I was really somewhat ashamed of my offence against good breeding.

I fully regretted having made the experiment, for I considered myself on the same level with a *gamin* who from his hiding-place hurls sunbeams reflected in his fragment of a mirror into the face of his neighbor with the intention of molesting him. However, I gradually opened my eyes to reconnoitre, unobserved, the situation, and seeing him busy again with his paper, I did not look into his face, but measured him, as it were, from head to toe.

He was a young man of about twenty-eight years, of imposing figure, with a strikingly handsome face, a high forehead, and eyes and mouth of the finest cut. He was dressed in black.

Now I renewed my game of flirting, but with quite a different intention. I wished to assist my memory, laboring desperately to find time, place and other circumstances to help me recall his features, which seemed strange to me no more; and while my memory struggled for deliverance, I looked sharply into his face for the purpose of making one last effort. Instantly he lifted his eyes, looked at me smilingly, got up from his seat, and came to my table.

"Pardon, monsieur," he said to me in French, "you seem greatly to exert your memory without being able to accomplish what you are laboring for. Perhaps I may be able to help you by breaking through the cloud which keeps me spell-bound in a misty vail, and thus withholds me from your spiritual eye."

"I am much obliged to you, sir, for your kindness, but this instant my ear hastens to the support of my memory. Those sonorous sounds still linger in my ears, ever since you called to me: 'We shall meet again!' You are surely Dr. Levin of P."

"Quite right."

"I bid you a hearty welcome!"

Pressing his hand, I added: "This time, dear doctor, I hope we shall have occasion to make our mutual acquaintance so thorough that in future it will not be necessary to make the scene of recognizing each other quite so dramatic."

"Come and see me this evening in the Hotel du Louvre, where we will have a pleasant chat for an hour or so; and though I am every moment awaiting orders for setting out on a new journey, I think I shall not leave Paris before the end of this week. Be sure to meet me this evening at seven o'clock, at the Hotel du Louvre."

He started for the door, when a footman entered, handing the doctor a letter. After reading it, the doctor said to the liveried man, who remained standing at a respectful distance:

"Is the carriage at the door?"

"At your service, sir."

"Then drive to the Madeline Church, and wait for me there."

"My friend," the doctor said to me, "it is now the second time that fate raises a separating wall between us; hardly do I enter into acquaintanceship with you, when I must leave you again. Prince O., whose court-physician I am, desires to start for London this evening. To my regret, I must again leave you, to make the necessary preparation for our journey. *Au revoir!*"

"And when shall I hear the story of—— ?"

"Come to the Hotel du Louvre, on the twenty-ninth of November, at seven P. M."

With these words, he cut off my question, and hurriedly walked away in the direction of the Madeline Church.

When I was alone, I drew my note-book out of my pocket, read the epitaph once more, and wrote in Hebrew letters on the margin: "Meeting with Dr. Levin, November 29th, this date corresponding with Kislev 15th, *jahrzeit* (anniversary of death) of the virgin Perl."

III.

In spite of the chilly mist covering the streets of Paris, I went on the appointed evening to the Hotel du Louvre, and arrived there at the time decided upon.

The doctor welcomed me most heartily in a rather dim room, and rolling a *tête-à-tête* in front of the mantelpiece, he bade me be seated and warm myself. He wished to look in his portfolio for some paper before sitting down by me.

Meanwhile I passed my time in looking at the fireplace, where logs were burning, and in listening to their crackling. They disseminated over the room a faint light and a pleasant, moderate heat. The logs lay in a mound of ashes, and the flames chased each other from log to log, as if to cover their retreat in case the accumulating embers should threaten to suffocate them. The flames had now left their path, by running into the ashes, and smoke arising from the half-burned wood took their place.

A faint jet of bluish light coming from the left side of the room now fell on my seat. In the corner, to my left, stood an aquarium of framed glass walls, surrounded by exotic plants hanging down like willows over a table made in rustic style. Above the middle of the aquarium was a basket of flowers, out of which creepers interlacing each other climbed down, dipping their sprigs into the water, and which, seen by the dim light, gave the whole the appearance of aquatics growing out of the water and forming a pyramid with its apex held together by the basket. The latter had the form of a ring, and was in reality intended as a round frame to hold a globe-shaped lamp of blue glass filled with transparent oil, on the surface of which a little blue flame swam around on a small boat of cork.

In the aquarium pretty little gold fish played around as if shone upon by the morning sun. It was the gleam of the lamp falling upon the water, which suffered not the little inhabitants of the aquarium to enjoy their evening rest. Sometimes they would come up to the surface and follow the movements of the little cork boat, as if they wanted to chase it; sometimes they would shoot down to the stony bottom and rest there a little while, only to renew their play once more.

It was the most elegant *jahrzeit* light I ever saw.

Meanwhile a violent puff of wind revived the smoking logs in the embers, and the flames threw their light upon the doctor, who laid the portfolio upon the table.

"I have found it at last," he whispered to me, putting a sheet of paper in the side-pocket of his coat. Then he sat down by me, and pressing my hand, he said:

"My friend, to-day four years ago I sat on this same spot, and, like you, looked upon the free play of the flames in this fireplace, while within me burned a glowing fire of love that threatened to consume me. I loved a girl with a passion not to be conceived by any mortal, a passion for which language has no expression.

"Perl Sanger was an exceptional girl. Like Calypso surrounded by her nymphs, she towered physically as well as mentally over all the girls I ever knew. Mother Nature, tired of her daily routine work of moulding after a well-regulated plan, seems to have wished, in a moment of caprice, to fashion a human being who was to be an exception to her kind; and in order that her stamp of perfection be remarkably visible on her forehead, she let a heavenly ray of light enter her soul, not only to thoroughly warm her heart with a holy fire, but also to illumine her spirit with a shining light, and thus endowed this God-kissed soul came into the world.

"In fact, Perl was at the age of sixteen a picture of perfection. Fancy a face combining Oriental with Hellenic beauty, a complexion as white as marble, deep azure eyes, nose and mouth of the most noble chiselling, an intellectual forehead, and raven-black hair of a luxuriance seldom to be seen, hanging over her neck in two long braids. Her figure and carriage——" here the doctor interrupted himself, rose from his seat, and, going to the background of the room, drew away a black cloth from a life-size oil portrait. I went near the picture, and after having lit the candelabra, the doctor came to my side, leaned his head over my shoulder, and looked sorrowfully at the excellent work of art.

"Look at this picture," he continued, "and you will have a better conception of her than you would gain from the most eloquent description that I could give."

The picture was remarkably beautiful, indeed. I stood contemplating it with childish curiosity, till the doctor took me by my arm and conducted me back to my seat. After covering the portrait with the black cloth, he again extinguished the lights, and sitting at my side, he continued:

"'The picture is, after all, nothing more than a faint copy of the original. What painter, even were he the most accomplished artist, could reproduce the brilliancy of her eyes when during our lessons she buried her piercing regard deep in my soul, stepping down to the fountain spring, as it were, from which to draw her instruction? I forgot to tell you that for a number of years I enjoyed the happiness of being her teacher.

"But I must hasten to continue my story, which I intend to tell simply, without ornamentation; and fearing I might run into the style of fiction, allow me to mention here, in a few words, that it did not take long before our hearts had learned how to understand, appreciate and love each other.

"A short time after receiving my doctor's diploma, I was at a reception party introduced to Prince O., and, to speak in the words of the Bible, having found favor in his eyes, I was nominated as his court-physician, on condition that I would be his travelling companion during two years.

"I gladly accepted the offer, for I was quite a young man, and wished to see the great world before laying the corner-stone of the structure of my little world wherein I intended that my Perl should establish an Eden for our mutual happiness.

"I travelled through Europe, Asia Minor and America, and you may imagine that I had access to the best of society. In my leisure hours, I visited hospitals and frequented the lectures of the most renowned professors in every land.

"I need not tell you that I kept up a lively correspondence with Perl. Her letters were my guiding-stars that shone before me on the career I had begun under such happy auspices. They excited my ambition to accumulate riches, glory, honors, and every earthly gift of fortune for the purpose of laying them at her feet.

"Her letters, every word of which inspired love, were dewdrops, refreshing and reviving my soul when fainting with ardent longing for her. These letters, my friend, are the only treasure that I have saved out of the ruins of a wrecked life; and though they are to-day but dried flowers, they still exhale the same fragrance, and since nothing keeps me alive but the remembrance of her, they have become for me a source of salvation that restores me, a cordial that protects me from despair.

" A thousand times I have read these letters over and over again, and have always derived from them comfort and peace. So does a man condemned to prison for life read the God-inspiring psalms day by day and hour by hour to divert his tormenting thoughts from this valley of tears and direct them to higher spheres of eternity.

"At the end of the second year, the return of the prince was postponed, contrary to his previous plans, and he resolved to stay a great part of the year in Southern France for the purpose of entirely restoring his broken health. Before starting on that second voyage, the prince graciously granted me one month's leave, and I started for P., after having informed Perl of my intended visit. The strange way in which I was received was an ominous augury of my future.

" You know that in small towns the railroad station forms a pleasure resort for the country people, where they like to see the trains coming and going, bearing travellers from all parts of the country. During the short stop, they contemplate the noise and bustle of the travelling folks, and consider themselves transported as if by magic to a large city, into the centre of life and activity. A whistle of the locomotive, the swollen stream recedes, and the peaceful quiet of the place is restored.

" While my train rolled slowly into the station, I looked through the car window at the assembled crowd to get a sight of Perl ; but my heart beat violently and my eyes refused their office. I tried to turn my head backward, but my strength was failing. I could only look in the direction the train was going. There—the car had stopped, and she must have noticed me—there she stood, leaning against a pillar; and, as if held by an invisible power, it was impossible for me to rise from my seat. I sat there as if struck by a flash of lightning. Suddenly I saw her close her hands around the pillar for fear of swooning. With one bound I stood by her, and I carried her half-fainting out of the crowd. By and by we felt more at ease, and our souls were freed from the fetters that a long absence had riveted around us, as we sat together speaking of the past and future.

"Only one drop of wormwood galled the cup of my joy, and that was the harrowing thought that Death was lurking at the entrance of my Eden. From the moment I had seen her leaning against the pillar, this painful thought never left me again, and I lacked the courage to call my medical skill to my assistance and by means of a diagnosis to announce her death-warrant, and perhaps mine. As often as I tried to do it, I could not prevail upon myself to procure the true evidence in her case. Whenever I looked into Perl's eyes, as often as I admired the noble but delicate form with which Nature had endowed her, as often as I was struck by the perfect maturity of her whole being at such a tender age, the suspicion that she might at any moment drop from the tree of life rose in my soul like a dark cloud.

"Our coming separation, however, did not cause us as much sorrow as we both anticipated. She soon recovered, looking quite blooming, and the healthy color which I noticed on her face the last days before my departure, sent a beam of hope into my troubled heart."

IV.

"About two years after this visit, I lived with the prince in Paris. He felt well, was quite restored, and manifested his desire to go to the *bal de l'opéra*. I, too, was in a cheerful mood, for in a very short time I expected to marry my darling, and I began already to count the days and hours of the expiring year, my leave being settled for January first. Besides, I received a letter from Perl, in which she assured me of her perfect health.

"After having given orders to the *valet de chambre* for two dominos, I made myself ready to accompany the prince to the Viscount B., where he wished to stay during the evening till the ball opened. We were just starting to leave the hotel when the prince had an attack, and I had to take him to bed. But the attack not being as severe as usual, he soon fell asleep, and I retired to my room at about seven o'clock.

"It was the twenty-ninth of November.

"I struck no light in my room, and seated myself before the fireplace on the same spot where we are now sitting. I tried to sleep, but in vain. I was in a feverish condition, continually staring at the flames, and I became the football of my fancy. At first I saw a red-hot pillar, on which little blue flames were running up and down, and Perl, as an apparition of fire, dancing around it, and when she stretched out her arms to embrace me the wrecked pillar fell over the apparition, and smoke rose from the burning ruins.

"New flames appeared as the logs were again ignited by the draft. Then I saw the background of the fireplace forming itself into a fiery tombstone. On its red-hot fire-sparkling surface appeared white lines, and on them the name *Perl Sanger;* immediately after, the words *fifteenth of Kislev,* all in Hebrew letters. These gradually disappeared, after these the white lines, and finally the tombstone fell crumbling into a heap of sparks, and an exhaling smoke rose in pyramidal form, ending at the highest point in a small blue flame.

"Awaking from this feverish torpor, I hastily struck a light, drew from the portfolio the sheet of paper I am now holding in my hand, and wrote on it Perl's epitaph in the Hebrew language. It flew, so to speak, out of my pen; there was no need for reflecting—I wrote against my will. The poem came to me by inspiration. Meter, scansion, rhyme—none of them were present to my mind. A higher power must have dictated the poem under my hand.

"When finished, I flung the pen upon the table.

"'Almighty God, be with us!'" I screamed aloud in despair, and fell back fainting on the chair. Out of this wretched position I was rescued by the *valet de chambre,* who had come to call me to the prince's bed.

"Without turning my face toward the mantelpiece, I flung the sheet of paper backward into the fire. The rest of the night I stayed with the prince, whose malady required my full attention, and I was glad that I could turn my thoughts in a different direction.

"At six in the morning, when I returned to my room the fire in the hearth had burned itself out, but the sheet lay across the fire-tongs; only the upper right-hand corner, as you see, was scorched by the fire, the epitaph remaining unimpaired. I recovered from my amazement, picked up the paper from the floor, and, without reading, put it into the portfolio.

"At ten I received the following telegraphic despatch:

"Perl died yesterday at seven o'clock, P. M.   More by letter.   SANGER."

*   *   *   *   *   *   *   *

"How do you explain the connection of your vision with the sad fact?" I asked, when the doctor had finished his story.

"How do I explain it?" said he, shrugging his shoulders. "Can or must we have an explanation for everything?"

"But you don't believe that ——?"

"I certainly believe the whole thing to be a mere accident, but I cannot help saying, in the words of Hamlet:

"There are more things in heaven and earth,
Than are dreamt of in your philosophy."

Like every respectable head of a family, old Jonathan Lot had gone to bed at nine o'clock, said with devotion his *sh'ma* prayer, drawn his night-cap over his ears, covered himself up to his chin with his feather-bed, and confided himself to the arms of Morpheus. He fell asleep and—dreamt. The god of dreams conducted him to the market-place and made him sit down on a bench, before the most frequented inn of the town. From his comfortable seat he inspected all the arriving guests. Among the arrivals he noticed an old man with a long white beard, who seemed to be looking for somebody. Jonathan rose from his seat, went to meet him, stretched out his hand, saluted him with a friendly *Sh'alom Alekem*, and asked him whether he was looking for somebody.

" Yes," answered the person addressed, " I am looking for Jonathan Lot."

" That is my name, and what can I do for you?"

" You will please accompany me to the Imperial and Royal Lottery Office, because I have to communicate a very important matter to you there."

" With the greatest pleasure," said Lot. "And to whom have I the honor of speaking?"

" I am the Prophet Elijah. I bring you three numbers which will, of a certainty, be drawn at the next drawing."

Jonathan bowed very low, thanked the prophet for his agreeable visit, and added :

"If you knew how long and how anxiously I have waited for your arrival, you would have come much sooner."

"You might have waited much longer for my arrival, for, to tell you the truth, my visit is not intended for you. The prize in question I will bestow as a dowry on your good daughter, Rachel, so as to put an end to her betrothal of so many years' standing, and to hasten her wedding-day. Your daughter wants five thousand florins; she shall have them this day week. You are an inveterate lottery-player, and have in vain squandered many a florin; but three numbers like those which I am going to whisper into your ear you have assuredly never put together. Now, listen. Take the tetragrammaton, the unpronounceable name of the Lord, the four letters of which give you the number twenty-six. If you now divide the name into halves the first two letters will give you the number fifteen; the remainder the number eleven."

They now stood in front of the lottery office, and Jonathan said to his companion:

"Excuse me, sir, for one minute; I will be back instantly."

He intended at once to insure his three numbers, but when he put his hand in his pocket, he found, to his dismay, that it was empty.

"*Shl'miel!*" shouted the Prophet Elijah, who had divined his intention, "what is your hurry? The drawing will not take place before the end of a week."

"You are quite right," replied Jonathan, "but till then I may have long forgotten your numbers."

"Let this be my care, for I have a good remedy for forgetfulness," said the Prophet Elijah. "Stand up

opposite me, close your eyes, and think of the unpronounceable name of the Lord, and, if your life is dear
to you, at no price open your eyes until I tell you to
do so."

Thus the prophet, who immediately afterward gave
Jonathan such a box on the ear that the poor man
opened his eyes, knocked his head against the head of his
bedstead, and—awoke.

The first thing Jonathan did—you, my dear reader,
would in his place have done the same—was to rub the
sleep from his eyes, rouse himself, and assure himself
whether he was awake or still dreaming. The next
thing he did was to feel with his hand whether the knock
on his head had produced a bump. Thanks to his thick
nightcap, however, his head had remained uninjured.

He could now occupy himself exclusively with his
lucky dream, and he began to think of the extent of his
stake, whether he would be satisfied with the prize of
five thousand florins, or increase it tenfold, whereby he
would win fifty thousand florins."

"I will find this out to-morrow," he soliloquized,
" when examining my pocket-book."

He then got out of bed very cautiously, so as not to
disturb from her sweet sleep his dear better-half, took
steel, flint and tinder, lit a candle, brought a piece of
chalk to write down the three numbers—being afraid
they might, by next day, slip from his memory—and,
after having looked a few moments about the room for
some appropriate place, selected the family altar—I
mean the large table which occupied the middle of the
room. On the table lay a small satchel, and near by
were written three numbers with a line underneath, evi-
dently prepared for summing up which somebody had

probably completed without writing down the amounts, he, doubtless, being a good mental arithmetician.

At any other time Jonathan would have considered these three numbers as a godsend, and would have risked a considerable stake thereon, but on such a happy night in which the Prophet Elijah, in person, had brought him his three numbers, and had with his own hand given him a box on the ear, he hardly noticed them, yea, he rubbed them out with his shirt-sleeve and wrote in their place eleven—fifteen—twenty-six, covered them with the satchel, blew out the light, and went to sleep again.

About four o'clock in the morning, when all in the house were in deep sleep, a man in travelling costume, holding a light in his hand, came from a room adjoining the one in which Jonathan Lot slept. Jonathan was snoring artistically, keeping time like a perfect musician. In order not to wake the respected head of the family, the man went on tiptoe toward the table, took the satchel in his hand, and noticing the three numbers he copied them in a little note-book. He then drew the house-key out of his pocket, blew out the light, and after he had pulled the door to from the outside he turned the key twice, and paced hurriedly away.

About an hour later, Nachmé, the worthy wife of our friend Jonathan, got out of bed and ushered in her working-day long before the sun made his tardy winter appearance. While her family was yet asleep, she was already busy sweeping the rooms, lighting the fires, and scrubbing the table and chairs. She scrubbed the table with fine, white sand, and thereafter carefully washed away every remaining speck, so that it looked as if it had been newly planed. By this means, she wiped out, without having the faintest idea of their significance, the last vestige of the Prophet Elijah's numbers, and, consequently, with them Jonathan's five or, perhaps, fifty thousand florins.

Meanwhile, Jonathan's snoring had subsided, and in its stead he had a second dream. Two dreams in one night are of ominous portent, as is well known to every child that has read in the Bible the history of Pharaoh and Joseph. Though the cows of the first dream be ever so fat, in the second dream lean ones will rise from the river, which will devour the fat ones, hides and horns. Well, our Jonathan had a second dream. This time he went directly to the lottery office to obtain his prize. Already from afar he noticed the three happy numbers emblazoned in gilded characters. He hastened his steps, but to his annoyance an old man, with a young lady on his arm, walked before him, barring his way; and though he tried to get ahead of them, they always succeeded in regaining the place in front of him, so that he could not advance. Arrived at the lottery office, both turned about face, and before him stood the Prophet Elijah with his daughter Rachel.

" Produce your lottery ticket!" shouted the prophet, with a voice of thunder.

Jonathan obeyed willingly, drawing the ticket out of his pocket ; but before he was aware of it the prophet had snapped it out of his hand, torn it in a thousand pieces, and cast them at his feet.

Jonathan began to weep piteously. Meanwhile, Nachmé, his wife, stood at his bedside, and, vigorously shaking him, said : " Jonathan, my love, why do you moan? Get up, dear! It is time to go to synagogue."

With one bound the good man jumped out of his bed, and his step was toward the table.

"*L'maan Hashem!*" (for God's sake) he exclaimed, quite bewildered; "wife, what have you done to my numbers? You have ruined me, yourself, and our children!"

II.

" Does heaven shower florin-pieces upon our heads, that you would again carry the money that ought to buy bread for our children to the lottery man?" scornfully asked Nachmé.

Old Jonathan cut a melancholy face, dressed hurriedly, and went to the synagogue with the *tallith* bag in his hand.

He had been in former years the richest, consequently the most respected man of his congregation. But not having devoted close attention and untiring industry to his business affairs; having, moreover, valued enjoyment higher than labor, it did not take him long to lose his considerable fortune. Shortly after his business crash, he had the further misfortune to lose his wife, who had given him an only daughter, known to us by the name of Rachel.

Naturally eager for the good things of life, and devotedly worshipping table delicacies and the best products of cookery, he condescended to take his cook as second wife, not only because she was a capital cook, and knew how to tickle his palate, but especially on account of the paltry sum of a few hundred florins which she had deposited in the savings-bank, and which, under his present circumstances, were not to be despised.

Nachmé, on her part, considered herself in this union

as a second Eugenie, Countess of Montijo, whom Napoleon
had elevated to the rank of empress in preference to all
the princesses of royal blood. Taken as a whole, Jonathan's second matrimonial venture might be called a
happy one, for both man and wife found in their union
the most perfect contentment. Nachmé was a virtuous
woman, presented her husband with five children, and,
by hard labor, not only supported her offspring, but even
her lazy husband, who depended upon her maintenance.
Jonathan led a life of idleness. His occupation con-
sisted of going to the synagogue three times a day,
regularly eating his three meals, smoking tobacco from
early morning to a late hour in the night, his sole business speculation being gambling in the lottery. This
was his whole aim and thought, and, so far from con-
tributing anything towards his family's wants, he even
spent the hard-earned money of his wife in lottery
tickets. ·

Nachmé established a *kosher* restaurant, and gave
board and lodging to travellers. When Rachel grew
older, she learned the millinery trade, and earned many
a florin which was contributed to the support of the
family.

Among the boarders was a young man, Moses Kirschner, who soon found favor in the eyes of the lovely
girl, and after some time an engagement between them
was the outcome of his devotion to her, which lasted a
number of years. It was not their fault that they did
not become man and wife ; the oath which Kirschner's
father had sworn by his life, that his son should marry
no girl who could not bring him a dowry of at least
five thousand florins, stood between them as a separating
wall.

But as Moses was not willing to give up his sweet-
heart, nothing was left to him but to wait and remain
Rachel's intended till at last the oath by his father's
life could do the old man no more harm; that is to say,
after his death.

To raise a dowry for his daughter Rachel, Jonathan
had made up all possible combinations of three numbers, composed of words either taken from his prayer-
book or from the Pentateuch, but thus far without any
result. The hoped-for prize of five thousand florins
would not come. There was always an insignificant
mistake, which brought his calculations to nought.
Sometimes the mutual position of two figures would
destroy his chances. He would put in eighty-seven,
and to his ill-luck seventy-eight would be drawn. Sometimes the difference of only one would bring about his
disappointment. He would put in thirty-five, while to
his bewilderment thirty-six would be drawn. "None
other but Satan," he would say, "could have played
me such a trick." However, every new disappointment
made him only more hopeful of future luck.

You may imagine the wretched state in which poor
old Jonathan found himself on the morning after that
eventful night when the Prophet Elijah had injured
him in such an outrageous manner. On his way home
from the synagogue, he looked the picture of despair.
Of his first dream, only the memory of the box on his
ear still remained to him, while the scraps of his lottery-
ticket, cast at his feet by the prophet, were the sole
remnants of his second. Of the numbers, however,
and of the mnemono-technical sign which the prophet
had given him, not the faintest trace was left in his
memory and, however hard he tried to think of them,

no other numbers came to his memory but those he found written under the satchel, and which he had rubbed out with his sleeve, in order to replace them by the numbers revealed to him by the prophet.

"Jonathan, my love," said his simple-minded wife, Nachmé, "I pray you, put this unfortunate dream out of your head, or you may get *meshugge* over it. God forbid! If it is the will of God, blessed be His name to make you happy, the prophet's numbers will be drawn, whether you play them or not."

"A great comfort, indeed, when these numbers will be drawn and another person win the prize," Jonathan remarked, angrily. "What a great joy it will be for us to see a stranger carrying home a bagful of money, while we shall remain poor, and my daughter's hair will get gray."

"And I insist upon it," maintained Nachmé, "that provided it is only God's will, blessed be His holy name, we will be made happy through these numbers, whether you play them or not."

Jonathan replied no more, but gazed in a superior manner at his wife, and drew his face into a pitying smile.

The day after the drawing, on which the drawn numbers were to be exhibited on the blackboard in front of the lottery office, Jonathan stayed away from morning service, for fear it might last too long, and recited his prayers at home. Without waiting for his breakfast, he went to the market-place and seated himself on the same bench where, in his dream, he had met the Prophet Elijah. Why he came there to wait with an empty stomach for numbers that could not concern him, nor bring him the least chance of gain, we do not know, nor could *he* have given any reason for it. But he sat there spellbound; and if he had any wish at all in his mind it was this: that if those so fatally forgotten numbers should make their appearance, his brain might become so paralyzed that he should not even then remember them, and so be spared the anguish the sight would bring him.

At last the lottery man appeared with the blackboard in his hand, and Jonathan could, without leaving his seat, see three red ribbon slips over which shone three numbers in gilt figures. At the sight of these numbers the entire dream flashed through his mind like a streak of lightning. "Woe unto me, God-forsaken," he exclaimed, striking his head with his fist; "how was it possible to forget the unpronounceable name of the Lord."

With closed eyes he sat there, unable to move from his place, as if rooted to the spot. At this moment a wagon came rattling up and stopped in front of the inn.

"What are you doing here so early, Reb Jonathan," exclaimed its occupant, alighting from the wagon and rousing the old man with a vigorous shake.

This time it was not the Prophet Elijah, but Moses Kirschner, the intended of his daughter Rachel. Instead of answering, Reb Jonathan stretched out his hand and pointed in the direction of the blackboard. Not a word came from his lips.

"Are you paralyzed with joy, that you are unable to utter a word?" asked Kirschner. Jonathan shook his head negatively, and tears rolled down his cheeks.

Meanwhile, Kirschner had more carefully looked at the gilt numbers, and an expression of surprised joy illumined his features, as he recognized the numbers which he had copied from the table on the morning of his departure.

"*Masol tov!*" he cried, turning to his future father-in-law. "This time you have won the prize, for I have played in the lottery the three numbers which, no doubt, my beloved Rachel had written on the table, covering them with my satchel so as to call my attention to them. Now she has her dowry of five thousand florins, and nothing is in the way to oppose our long-hoped-for union."

When good Nachmé heard this happy news, she said:

"Well, Jonathan, my love, was I not right when I said that if God, may His name be blessed, desires to make you happy, you will win the prize, whether you play or not?"

Two months after these happy events, Rachel was conducted to the *huppah*, after her father had, *pro forma*, counted down and handed over five thousand florins to his son-in law in the presence of old Kirschner.

While the wedding guests were sitting merrily at the feast, Jonathan Lot slipped away unobserved to the market-place, to try once more on this joyful day, which surely must bring luck, the numbers the Prophet Elijah had brought him. As an old practitioner, he believed he he had learned from experience that the same numbers could not possibly be drawn twice in succession, not even after quite long intervals. According to his idea, not even Elijah had it in his power to perform such a miracle. He, therefore, played *solo*, *i. e.*, he selected from the three numbers the largest one (twenty-six) which represented the full name of Jehovah. To his utter discomfiture, eleven—fifteen—twenty-six again made their appearance on the blackboard, but this time neither in gilded figures nor ornamented with red ribbons, for he had neglected to play them, and the drawn number twenty-six, which got him a prize—a mere pittance of fourteen florins—a lottery man did not deem worth ornamenting.

Since that day, Jonathan Lot has given up lottery gambling.

VANITY AND VANITIES.

Uncle Moses was a famous Talmudist, and a casuist of the first order.

He possessed, moreover, the means of devoting himself entirely to his favorite studies, for in his bookcase there was a little drawer containing a bundle of coupons.

There was no question in the Talmud ever so puzzling, which he could not answer satisfactorily.

But there was one question not contained in the Talmud which neither he nor his contemporaries were able to answer; it was this: "Why did not Uncle Moses find a helpmeet for himself?"

On his sixtieth birthday, a feeling of loneliness in God's great world having overcome him, he began to think of a speedy union with mother earth, and therefore ordered his grave clothes, bought a plot of ground for an eternal resting-place for his mortal remains, and even his tombstone.

Whether he was the author of his own epitaph, or whether some friendly versifier composed it for him, is a question which history may never be able to solve, but this much is certain; that, like most Hebrew epitaphs, it was written in the well-known exuberant style which made it read like an ode. Indeed, were all the Hebrew testimonials which are engraved on the tombstones not taken *cum grano salis*, one might come to the conclusion that all those that sleep in the dust must have been in their life-times either demi-gods, or at least saints.

Uncle Moses did not only read the flattering description of his person, but he even passed many an hour with the engraver, watching him closely while he chiselled letter after letter, covered them with black paint, and gilded his name, Moses Moos. He felt as happy as an urchin who watches his teacher while writing, at the closing school-hour, a "good ticket" that ranks him at the head of his class.

This stone stood many a year in the house for the reception of the dead, and the members of his congregation had occasion to read its inscription at every funeral, for it remained on exhibition no less than fifteen years, since Uncle Moses attained the advanced age of seventy-five years.

Literally translated, the inscription would read thus:

"And the Lord called Moses to himself; in order that he might behold the glory of the Most High, find shelter under the wings of His divine Majesty, and enjoy the fruits of his deeds of piety. For Moses is a servant of the Lord, in all his house is he faithful. He is the head of his congregation and an ornament in Israel. Behold, such is the honest, pious, and learned Rabbi Moses Moos, died on the —— day of the month of ——, in the year ——. May his soul be bound in the bond of eternal life."

Had Uncle Moses, like his namesake, been endowed with the gift of prophecy, he would surely not have left even the blank for the date.

"After all, it is better not to be a prophet," he used to say. "The missing date can easily be inserted before the stone is erected. But fancy for a moment if the stone had the date on it; how would I feel the last week of my stay on earth, when God, blessed be He, will call me away! A most miserable situation it would be for me to sit watching and counting, minute after minute, the sands of time running down the hour-glass!"

One day, Uncle Moses received at his house an inti-mate friend, a former schoolmate, by the name of El'azar Fleckeles, who had come from Prague for the purpose of visiting his parents' grave. As the friends passed through the mortuary house, they came to a standstill in front of the famous tombstone, and El'azar read its inscription.

" Well, how do you like it?" asked Uncle Moses.

" Instead of an answer, allow me to tell you a story," replied Fleckeles:

Once upon a time there came two journeymen tailors to Prague.

Natives of Eibenshutz, in Moravia, they had travelled together during six years, found employment in different cities, and wished now to settle permanently in Prague. At the city gate a policeman stopped them, and asked for their passports. He read the description of the first. " Nose, pointed; eyes, brown; forehead, high;" at a glance he noticed that his nose was flat, his eyes gray, and his forehead low.

" Man, how did you come in possession of this fraudu-lent passport?" exclaimed the policeman, angrily.

" Captain," replied the tailor, tremblingly, " I come from Eibenshutz, but the seat of my county government being in Krummau, I got my passport through an agent. He alone is responsible for the description of my physiognomy; he must have drawn it up from memory, as I was not present when it was made out."

The policeman, accepting this very reasonable excuse,

handed him a permit of residence in the capital of Bohemia.

Now came the second tailor's turn.

When the policeman perused his passport, he found under the heading: Special distinguishing marks, *none*. The tailor had, however, just on the tip of his nose, a wart of the size of a hazel-nut, a tuft of hair growing on top of it, looking like a little woody hill.

"Man!" said the policeman, "how could the magistrate who wrote your passport have overlooked your wart? Were you, too, absent when he wrote it?"

"Oh no, I beg your pardon, I was present, but I felt happy when I saw that he took no notice of my defect, which I tried to conceal as best I could. Is it not sad enough to have a wart just in the middle of one's face? Must a description of it also appear in one's passport?"

"Your passport is fraudulent, and you are a fraud," cried the policeman. "You were present when your passport was made out, and it was your bounden duty to call the magistrate's attention to your wart, but having neglected to do so, you will have to be fined."

"With this passport," continued Fleckeles, pointing at the tombstone, "you will never get a permit of residence in the world to come. I ask you, my friend, are your vanity and craving for self-praise not like loathsome warts, which will have to be extirpated before you can think of considering this picture of yours as taken from life? Will braggadocio never cease, not even here? Dare they engrave the lie in the tombstone, I might say the milestone, which stands on the line dividing this world from the next?"

* * * * * * * * *

Three days after Fleckeles' departure, Uncle Moses

stood again in the stone-cutter's yard, watching the heavy, continuous strokes the hammer dealt on the head of the engraver's chisel for the purpose of cutting out the black warts, and rendering the stone a *tabula rasa.*

* * * * * * * * *

After Uncle Moses' death, when they opened the drawer of his book-case, the following epitaph was found among his papers:

Here lies
Moses Moos,
Died on the —— day of ——.
In the year ——.
Peace be to his ashes.

A FALSE TURN.

The people of Bumsle are, strictly speaking, no fools; should some sort of folly, however, meet them half-way, they would, instead of stepping aside, be more likely to run after it, and not stop in their course before they had picked it up.

Sam Passy, a good-natured but narrow-minded sort of a fellow, had never crossed the boundaries of his little native place, although Spring had, at its yearly appearance, more than fifty times invited him to visit the surrounding field and meadows. He stubbornly clung to his lane and little shop on the market-place.

He had a thousand-and-one excuses. He was no migratory bird, did not like a change, was afraid of getting home-sick, favored the very dust of his lane, and last, but not least, considered it ungrateful to absent himself even for a few hours from his birthplace, in which he had a thriving business. Spring might have come and gone fifty times more without having the least effect upon him, and Sam Passy might have gone to his fathers in peace, and been buried at a good old age, without ever having seen Prague, the capital city of his province.

But it happened one Sabbath, while in synagogue, that he had a neighbor in his pew, a man from Prague, who, on a *shnorring* tour through Bohemia and Moravia, sojourned in Bumsle. Though preaching on a common Sabbath was not yet introduced, *Mussaph* service used, nevertheless, in the good old times, to last for more than two hours. Now, I ask, is it possible to pray devotionally during two consecutive hours? The guest quite naturally devoted some time to talking to our Sam Passy, and he entertained him most pleasantly, relating to him many a legend of the "great Rabbi Loeb" of Prague, and of the *golem* into whose nostrils he breathed the spirit of life, and whom he slew again on Sabbath eve, and flung afterwards into the garden of the *altneuschul*, where up to this day he still lies, and may be seen changed into a heap of mud.

From that moment Sam had nothing but the *golem*. in his eye.

Coming home from *schul* in a feverish excitement, he felt an appetite of quite an unusual degree. He ate that day twice as much as on an ordinary Sabbath: half a *kugel*, plus half a *zwetschen-bobele*, and after his Sabbath nap, when rubbing the sleep from his eyes, he felt as if his stomach were henceforth able to enjoy a rest of forty days and forty nights. After such a preparation he thought he could, like the Prophet Elijah, undertake a very, very long journey, and courageously meet any adventure, and were the *golem* resuscitated from his mud-heap, running wild in the streets of Prague, he would not fare any better under his hands, than the priests of Baal under the mighty blows of the Prophet Elijah.

"Leah, my dear," said he to his wife, "this evening, as soon as the *havdoloh* wax light is smothered in the wine, you will bring down my stick and lantern, for I have a long journey before me. I will walk all night, and arrive to-morrow morning in Prague."

"To Prague, afoot? Are you, God forbid, out of your senses?" exclaimed Leah, quite beside herself. "Why just on Sabbath evening? One would think you were a messenger hired to take a message to Prague, to be delivered in the morning. If you wish to see Prague, why not rather select a week-day, when you could perhaps get a free ride, or else travel in a stage coach?"

"Let other people talk reason to women, *I* will not," replied Sam, angrily. "Had I told you, Leah, I should start to-morrow, you would in all probability have objected. Why not rather start immediately after *havdoloh*, since I could have the whole Sunday for myself. Pray do not disturb my *oneg Shabbes* (Sabbath delight). No more objections, if you please, for it is my firm wish to be in Prague to-morrow morning."

Leah kept silent. Another objection would have produced the effect of a red flag on a fighting bull.

Even after *havdoloh*, when Sam, cleaning his lantern in a hurry, knocked in one of the panes, a very ominous sign for a Sabbath evening undertaking, even then Leah uttered not a word. She stood on her door-sill and repeated the *yeborech'cho* (blessing) till her husband was out of her sight.

Until midnight everything went straight with our traveller, who passed his time pleasantly, singing liturgical songs.

Midnight came, and with it an unexpected perplexity. He had then arrived where the road branched off like a fork, one path leading to the right, the other to the left.

What now? He deliberated a little while, and setting his lantern on the ground, he looked now in one, now in another direction. "All ways lead to Rome," he soliloquized, in the words of the old proverb, and lifted his lantern with the intention of taking the road to his right hand, when all of a sudden a draught blew out his light. Quickly he turned about for the purpose of protecting his lantern against the wind with the whole breadth of his body, and possibly reviving his light by painfully blowing into the fainting glow of the wick. In vain. All his efforts were fruitless.

This little mishap made him entirely forget that he had turned "about face," and carrying his lantern under his arm, he marched on, looking neither to right nor left, but straightforward on the old road. Did I say "forward?" I beg pardon, I should have said he marched, without suspecting it, straight back to Bumsle.

"All ways lead to Rome," he comforted himself once more. "And suppose I should arrive an hour or two later than at six o'clock?" Cheerfully he marched on through the second half of the night, following the road that led him direct to Bumsle.

Morning dawned.

A lovely air fanned into his face the sweet fragrance ascending from the meadows, and the merry songs of the birds sounding from the woods made the world appear rose-colored to him. Over the horizon lay a dense fog.

"Perhaps I am nearer Prague than I thought an hour ago," he said to himself. "This fog appears to me like a huge, gray, silk night-cap drawn over the head of the city which sleeps late in the day. On my arrival I may be the first to wake her from her sleep."

And when the first rays of the sun had frightened away the misty vapors, a city lay in reality before him, and Sam Passy could not find words enough to express his admiration of the beautiful steeple that, like a slender oak, grew out of the church roof.

"How great are thy works, O Lord!" he exclaimed, agreeably surprised, "just the same as in Bumsle. Isn't it wonderful! Our steeple and this are as like each other as two eggs."

Arrived in the midst of the market-place, his eyes fell on the statue of St. John Nepomuk (the Bohemian St. Patrick). Horror-stricken, he halted before the huge stone figure.

"Wonders never cease!" he cried out. "I could swear that the Bumsle Nepomuk and this are twin brothers."

But the Jews' lane with the little synagogue utterly disappointed him.

"And this is the famous *altneuschul* all the world talks so much about, this little structure, which is not a bit larger than ours? Is it not just the same as in Bumsle? Really they ought to be ashamed of themselves, those Jewish nabobs of Prague, who would not spend more money on their synagogue than we in Bumsle."

Not far from the synagogue he stopped in front of a house that called to his mind his own cosy little abode in Bumsle. He could not resist the temptation of entering, and ran up one flight of stairs.

Leah Passy was an excellent housekeeper as well as a very pious woman, and her room was, at that hour, already in perfect order. She was just reading her morning prayers out of a goodly sized *tephillah*, and at the same time watching a porringer in which the milk for her breakfast was boiling; thus devoting soul and body jointly to the fear of the Lord, and the fear lest her milk run over.

At the unexpected sight of her husband she was

unable to find words to express her surprise, but
had she even found any, she could not have uttered
them just now without committing a grave offence, that
of interrupting herself in the middle of the *eighteen
benedictions.*

This circumstance gave her husband the floor, and he
intended to use it freely for giving vent to his angry
feelings. But the introductory powerful knock with
his fist on the table, having tumbled over the porringer
and spilt the milk, his temper softened at the sight of
the mess he had made.

" Wife," said he, " I do not wish to quarrel over spilt
milk, but tell me one thing, is Bumsle not good enough
for you anymore, that you run after me to Prague?"

HOW MENDELSSOHN BARTHOLDY FARED IN HEAVEN.

Felix Mendelssohn Bartholdy was dead, and carried to his untimely grave, mourned by numerous admirers of his genius. But while mankind delighted in the enduring monuments of his art in the three works—"Œdipus," "Paulus" and "Elijah"—Euterpe's son had to undergo many an unpleasant humiliation on his way to heaven.

His natural inclination to the classics stimulated him to look at first for the heaven of the Greeks, an undertaking fraught with many a great difficulty. For, in order to get there, he had to search for Charon, whom the gods appointed as ferry-man to convey the souls of the departed in a boat across the Stygian Lake. Unfortunately, on his sudden departure from this world, Mendelssohn had forgotten to take along his spectacles, which he could not very well do without on account of his near-sightedness, and, surrounded by the thick, infernal darkness covering the shores of that lake, he had the greatest trouble in finding the ferry-man. When he at last met him he discovered, to his dismay, that he had not even taken his pocket-book to pay the passage. But chance sent a Berlin art-critic in his way, who relieved him of his embarrassment by lending him an *obolus* to pay his fare.

Presently, he stood before Jupiter's throne and applied for admission.

"What! You wish to abide with me?" asked Zeus,

"but I don't know you; never heard of you. Have you any letters of introduction?"

"My name is Mendelssohn Bartholdy. I am the composer of 'Œdipus.' Surely Sophocles, Melpomene's most distinguished son, must have heard of me."

At a sign from the god, Hermes went for Sophocles.

The proud Grecian measured him from head to toe; then he said, mockingly: "Mendelssohn does not sound like a Greek name, nor is Berlin in the Peloponnesus. Moreover, a person not born on the islands of the Archipelago we have at all times considered a barbarian. Why, then, do you wish to intrude upon us?" Thus spake Sophocles, who immediately signed to Hermes to show the applicant back to the gate.

Mendelssohn paced away slowly, his head bowed down in meditation, as if a new musical composition were occupying his mind. When he again lifted his head, he stood before another gate, and asked to be admitted.

"You wish to be received here," said St. Peter; "who are you?"

"I am the composer of 'Paulus,' an oratorio which the whole Christian world considers a master-work of church-music."

"'Paulus!' 'Paulus!'" said St. Peter, shaking his head, "that name has a suspicious odor of Protestantism. I am very sorry that I cannot accede to your demand. As long as this hand holds the key of heaven, no Protestant shall ever enter at this gate." St. Peter closed the gate and left him standing without.

On the opposite side a gate stood ajar, through which a tired wanderer had just been admitted, and Bartholdy availing himself of the opportune moment, made a sign to the gate-keeper that he should admit him.

"What is your name?" asked father Abraham, with a friendly mien.

"My name is Mendelssohn Bartholdy; I am the composer of Elijah," he replied, visibly embarrassed.

"Bartholdy! Bartholdy!" said father Abraham, emphatically pronouncing this name. "What is the meaning of Bartholdy? No true Jew would bear a name like Bartholdy. This is no Biblical name; in fact, in the whole Jewish heaven there is not one called that way. Nor do I understand what you mean by claiming to have set to music the prophet Elijah. I know King David set his psalms to music. But Elijah in music! What a strange thing, very strange indeed!"

"But I told you my name was *Mendelssohn* Bartholdy," rejoined the composer, laying stress on his first name.

"I have no objection against Mendelssohn; this name I know quite well. Every child has heard of Moses Mendelssohn, and in heaven he is enrolled under the name of Rabbi Moshe ben Mena'hem, of Dessau. But Bartholdy, Bartholdy—no, no, my child!" continued Abraham, sympathetically, "you are mistaken, this is not your place; in our Jewish heaven you will never feel at home."

Thus three times disappointed in his expectations, Mendelssohn Bartholdy stood helplessly at the entrance of the Jewish heaven, not knowing which way to turn. He would not retrace his steps in the direction he came from, because he was unwilling to pass by the gates at which he had been so scornfully treated. So he marched aimlessly forward.

After having wandered for a long time, it seemed to him as if he heard a chorus. In very truth, his fine musical ear did not deceive him. The further he went the more distinctly he recognized a song composed in the style of a fugue.

"Surely that is my own composition," he cried out, joyfully. "I can now distinctly hear even the text; it is my Turkish drinking song:

> Setze mir nicht, du Grobian,
> Den Krug so derb vor die Nase;
> Wer Wein bringt, seh' mich freundlich an,
> Sonst trübt sich der Elfer im Glase.

"Truly, a heaven full of earthly enjoyments, where they sing, drink and love, can be no other than the Mohammedan. Well, let me try."

When he entered, the last sounds of the song had died away. Mohammed, receiving him with a friendly *Salom Alekhem*, asked:

"Who are you?"

"My name is Mendelssohn Bartholdy, the composer of the drinking-song which made you all so merry. As a reward for my composition, grant me admission into your heaven!"

Then the prophet embraced him, saying: "If you are willing to live in my heaven, it shall be open to you as often as you come"

TOO LATE.*

And thou shalt rejoice in thy feast (Deut. xvi : 14).

For fully seven years had Reb Kalman, far from his wife and children, led a solitary life in the Russian coronation city of Moscow, where he had made all his purchases, and still he could not make up his mind to return to his family. At thought of the immense distance that lay between him and his loved ones, and which he must traverse to see them again, he turned from the dangerous project whenever he contemplated it, for at that time no railroads as yet existed. Moreover, he could fully rely on the energy and ability of his wife, who, during his absence, not only ably conducted her household, but looked thoroughly to the management of the business as well. Indeed, Bitja, such was his wife's name, was as much in the store as in her house, and was ably supported therein by her eldest daughter, who had been a girl of ten when her father left them. This excellent mother taught her girls herself, instructed them in all kinds of feminine handiwork, and at the same time saw to it that her boys attended school regularly, as, indeed, she trained all her children carefully in virtue and the fear of God.

But it happened one day that Reb Kalman received from his wife Bitja a letter, in which she informed him that she had chosen for her oldest daughter, who had now blossomed into a beautiful maiden, a splendid

---

* Founded on a Hebrew poem.

youth to be her husband. "Our future son-in-law,"
thus she wrote, "is descended from a family that has
produced many rabbis, widely known and famous in all
Russia and Poland, and the young man has studied and
memorized no less than five hundred pages of *Gemora*.
The betrothal will take place on the last day of the
approaching *Succoth* feast, and the *Mechuttonim* will be
our guests for three days—you are aware that in this
year *Sabbath B'reshith* follows immediately on *Simchath
Torah*. They will bring the *chosson* with them, so that
the young people may become acquainted with each
other.

This unexpected and joyful news effectually roused
the dilatory father and husband from his lethargy.

"I shall come without delay," he wrote to Bitja, "and
will beat off my *Hoshaanoth* in our synagogue this year.
For each of you I will bring presents that shall rejoice
your hearts."

And in very truth Reb Kalman left the eastern
capital of Russia as early as the last third of the month
of *Ellul*, and, seated in a wagon drawn by three powerful horses, soon left the spires of the historic city far
behind him. He calculated that, in order to make this
long journey, he would require at least a month's time,
all the more as continuous rains had made the roads
well-nigh impassable. Nor did he suffer from a lack of
adventures during his travels. Here and there the
rivers had left their beds and flooded the flat country.
From either side larger and smaller bridges, that the
floods had broken from their fastenings, went floating
by, and were carried far over the country by the turbu-
lent waters. Trembling for his life, he was, in several
cases, obliged to cross a bridge that swayed danger-

ously beneath him, and threatened momentarily to be
in its turn torn away by the destructive floods. But
how trifling to the pious man seemed all the dangers he
had already passed and those he had still to encounter,
compared to the heartache he experienced at the
thought that he might be unavoidably compelled to
neglect his religious duties. Where, while under way,
should he in the impending *Teshubah* days, rise early
enough for *Slichoth?* Where on his journey, make
Tashlich? Where procure a snow-white rooster with
which to whirl the *Kapporah* around his head? It is
true that he was not forced to give up these religious
duties entirely. Several *Slichoth* mornings, on the
feast of *Rosh Hashanah*, on the day of *Yom Kippur* and
the first days of *Succoth*, he would not be deterred from
stopping in such places where there were Jewish con-
gregations; and thus the good man spent an entire
month among strangers, in miserable taverns, and rested
at night on filthy straw.

Only the thought of his loved ones served to give him
new strength to endure these tremendous hardships.
During the long nights, when in a half-waking, half-
sleeping state, he stretched his tired limbs on the poor
straw in his wagon, his fancy would picture to him his
comfortable home. He would see his wife surrounded
by their children, his future son-in-law, all the friends
of his boyhood's days assembled in honor of his coming
and overjoyed to see him again. They all stood around
the table, decked with snowy linen, ready to sit down
to the feast when bidden to do so by Bitja. Savory
viands smoked in the well-filled dishes, dumplings light
as air floated about in the golden-yellow soup; the roast,
well-seasoned with garlic and onions, diffused an appe-

tizing odor; the braided twists of finest wheaten flour were thickly bestrewn with poppy-seeds; the cabbage hid toothsome chestnuts in its depths, and a mighty dish of almond cakes graced the centre of the board. Well he knows what an excellent cook his Bitja is, the ideal surroundings which his fancy creates put him into quite a festive state of mind, and he thinks no less than that at this moment he already literally complies with the Mosaic law: "Thou shalt rejoice in thy feast."

And yet, in reality, the good man has not the least cause to rejoice, for a drizzling, incessant rain will not allow his tired eyelids to close in much-yearned-for sleep, and his wagon is moving slowly along through a swamp that arrests the wheels in their progress for minutes at a time. Now the horses refuse to move at all, and will not be persuaded to go on in spite of the driver's curses; anon the reins break, or a wheel is lost and must be replaced by another. At times he rouses himself and lends his voice to strengthen that of the driver. The horses bestir themselves for a space, but soon relapse into their former pace, and they creep along again like snails. Alas, the hours fly like winged birds, while the road and the deep mud through which the vehicle toils so painfully stretch away into the limitless distance. Who will blame poor Reb Kalman that his long-tried patience threatens to give way, and that at the thought of not being with his loved ones on *Simchath Torah* the hair of his head erects itself with horror! Brooks rise, billows roll, nights pass, days vanish. Will the countless taverns never come to an end?

On *Hoshaana Rabbah* night he put up at a tavern that lay but six miles distant from his native town. He sat there in a small, dark room, more like a cellar than a sleeping apartment, absorbed in the perusal of the book Deuteronomy and the *Tikkun ha-Zohar*. The flame of a thin tallow candle, that was wound about with paper to prevent its slipping down the large tube of the candlestick, diffused a faint light which served rather to heighten the shadows than illumine the room. Gloomy shadows played about the walls, and gloomier ones rose in his soul, while, in these dark and cheerless surroundings, the thought of his family and home overcame him. But how was the poor man startled when, accidentally raising his eyes to the ceiling, he beheld there his own grotesquely lengthened shadow! To see one's own shadow is nothing uncommon and has nothing frightful connected with it. But in the *Hoshaana Rabbah* night to see one's own shadow without the head thereunto appertaining, that, to the *Chassidaic* Jew, is a matter of life and death, and equal to a sentence of death pronounced by the Judge of judges on him who thus sees himself shadowed.

However, good Reb Kalman could not see the shadow of his head for the perfectly natural reason that, just where it should have been, a massive black cross-beam on the ceiling cut it off from the trunk, and thus withdrew it from the eyes of the poor man who now trembled in every limb. "*Shema Yisroel*," he cried out in terror, "has my last hour come, and must I perish here so near my home, and yet so far from wife and children, with none near me to close my eyes?"

Early on the following morning, after he had completed his devotions and beaten the willow branches until they were denuded of all their leafy garb, he sprang quickly into his wagon and continued his journey.

The rain had ceased, the heavens showed a cheerful face, the clouds had disappeared, and slowly the sun beamed forth in all its radiance. Into Reb Kalman's heart, also, there stole a ray of hope which dispelled the dark shadows and violent emotions of the past night, and he made new exertions to reach his home, which now lay only three miles distant. But, alas, the minutes fly away, the hours depart, the horses are tired and exhausted, and make but little progress, while the sun is no longer distant from the ocean where it takes its nightly bath. In the natural course of things, Reb Kalman can never, under existing conditions, hope to reach his home ere the breaking in of the holiday. But now comes delusive hope and whispers into the ear of the credulous Chassid: "May not a miracle be done for thy sake? May not, for thy sake, the distance be diminished, as of old for the patriarch Jacob on his way from *Beer Sheba* to *Charan*? Why may not the sun stand still for thee, as once it did for Joshua?"

Alas, miracles no longer happen, for even heaven and earth are no longer so near each other as in the good old time. No, the mountain will not come to Mahomet. Reb Kalman's native town does not stir from its place and run to meet him in order to save the steps for his tired horses. Alas, again the sun sinks rapidly to rest, the horses trudge wearily onward with heavy tread and long-stretched necks, Reb Kalman in the apathy of despair lies in his wagon like a corpse in its coffin, now and then raising his eyes to heaven, and trembling as with the ague. The shades of evening descend on the valley. He is but a mile away from his home. But now he breaks into sobs and moans, and cries imploringly: " Pray for me, ye hills and mountains, stay the sun in its course, delay it but for two short hours !"

In vain his glances search the hills and mountains. The hills are deaf, the mountains have no ears. Lower and lower sinks the sun and approaches the edge of the heavens.

Nor is it of any avail that Reb Kalman shouts himself hoarse in the attempt to hasten the progress of the wagon. The horses do what they can, but their feet sink deeply into the mud—there is no hope that they will reach the town before midnight.

One by one the stars come out and send down their faint silvery rays. Curses on you, ye rulers of the night! Cursed be your coming and going; why must ye come forth from your hiding place so early just on this day, and cast your pale light, as if in scorn, at my face?

Reb Kalman arrived at a village but half an hour distant from his home. The peace of the Sabbath reigned here. Lights gleamed from the windows of festively illuminated rooms, for *Yom Tob* had already held its entrance. From one house there proceeded the sounds of the worshippers who were assembled for the evening's devotions. Plainly Reb Kalman discerned the voice of the reader as he intoned the *Borkhu*, and in full and strong chorus came the response, " Blessed be the Lord who is blessed for evermore !" Help was no longer possible.

" Turn about and drive to the tavern. We cannot go any further and will remain here over *Yom Tob*," cried Reb Kalman to the driver, in a voice of utter exhaustion.

" Where does our father stay? Has he met with a misfortune?" Thus cried the members of Reb Kalman's family, as he failed to make his appearance, and

wrung their hands in despair. The joy of the feast
was gone. *Simchath Torah* turned into *Yom Kippur.*
Tortured by fear and anxiety poor Bitja fell into a dangerous illness, and in consequence thereof, the young
man was not presented to his future bride. Scarcely
had, at the departure of *Yom Tob*, the *Havdoloh* been
made, than the *Mechuttonim* mounted their wagon and
drove away in haste as if the enemy were at their back.
And, alas, the poor *shadken !* The dainty morsel he had
almost held between his teeth was ruthlessly torn away.

In the early morning hours of the following Sunday,
when Reb Kalman entered his room he found his wife
almost dying, and beside her, his daughter sitting in
mute despair. At sight of him she broke into a piteous
cry. Was it for him or for her bridegroom? Who
would dare in such a heart-breaking moment to pry
into the most sacred thoughts of a maiden's and daughter's heart?

Fie upon thee, *Techum Shabbos,* how could you bring
down so much misery on this poor family ! How could
you convert a happy home into a house of mourning ;
blight the life of a young girl, despoil a rose ere it had
bloomed ?

Poor Reb Kalman! Your vision in the *Hoshaana
Rabbah* night was fulfilled. You had really no head,
else, despite stars, festive lights, and sounds of *Borkhu,*
you would have hastened to your dear ones on the eve
of the holiday, and saved them from all the ensuing
heartache. Had you learned something proper, had
you had but the shadow of a head on your shoulders,
you needs must have known that *Techum Shabbos* is
only a rabbinical regulation, while " Thou shalt rejoice
in thy feast " is a distinctly prescribed Mosaic law.

PUBLICATIONS

JEWISH PUBLICATION SOCIETY OF AMERICA.

Membership Dues: $3.00 per Annum.

The American Jewish Publication Society, which has just issued its third work, the first volume of the new English translation of Graetz's "History of the Jews," was organized in Philadelphia in June, 1888, with a view to publishing books on the religion, literature, and history of the Jews, and of fostering original work by American scholars in these subjects. It has branches in a number of large cities, with about 3,000 members, and is managed by an Executive Committee and a Publication Board. Its previous issues have been Mrs. Magnus' "Post-Biblical History," and "Think and Thank," a story for the young. A special series of brochures has been begun, the first being devoted to a reprint of a pamphlet on the Russian question, to be followed by original and selected papers in Jewish literature and research, akin somewhat in style to *Chambers' Miscellany.* . . . The Publication Committee is in active correspondence with writers abroad and at home for fresh material, and its forthcoming works are likely to prove attractive. Financially the Society is in good condition, and it pays its writers handsomely.—*Nation* (New York).

OUTLINES OF JEWISH HISTORY.

From the Return from Babylon to the Present Time, 1890.

With Three Maps, a Frontispiece and Chronological Tables.

By LADY MAGNUS.

Revised by M. FRIEDLÄNDER, Ph. D.

OPINIONS OF THE PRESS.

The entire work is one of great interest; it is written with moderation, and yet with a fine enthusiasm for the great race which is set before the reader's mind —*Atlantic Monthly.*

We doubt whether there is in the English language a better sketch of Jewish history. The Jewish Publication Society is to be congratulated on the successful opening of its career. Such a movement, so auspiciously begun, deserves the hearty support of the public.—*Nation* (New York).

Of universal historical interest.—*Philadelphia Ledger.*

Compresses much in simple language.—*Baltimore Sun.*

Though full of sympathy for her own people, it is not without a singular value for readers whose religious belief differs from that of the author.—*New York Times.*

One of the clearest and most compact works of its class produced in modern times.—*New York Sun.*

The Jewish Publication Society of America has not only conferred a favor upon all young Hebrews, but also upon all Gentiles who desire to see the Jew as he appears to himself.—*Boston Herald.*

We know of no single-volume history which gives a better idea of the remarkable part played by the Jews in ancient and modern history.—*San Francisco Chronicle.*

A succinct, well-written history of a wonderful race.—*Buffalo Courier.*

The best hand-book of Jewish history that readers of any class can find.—*New York Herald.*

A convenient and attractive hand-book of Jewish history.—*Cleveland Plain Dealer.*

The work is an admirable one, and as a manual of Jewish history it may be commended to persons of every race and creed.—*Philadelphia Times.*

Altogether it would be difficult to find another book on this subject containing so much information.—*American* (Philadelphia).

Lady Magnus' book is a valuable addition to the store-house of literature that we already have about the Jews.—*Charleston (S. C.) News.*

We should like to see this volume in the library of every school in the State.—*Albany Argus.*

A succinct, helpful portrayal of Jewish history.—*Boston Post.*

Bound in Cloth.   **Price, postpaid, $1.25.**

"THINK AND THANK."

A Tale for the Young, Narrating in Romantic Form the
Boyhood of Sir Moses Montefiore.

WITH SIX ILLUSTRATIONS.

By SAMUEL W. COOPER.

OPINIONS OF THE PRESS.

A graphic and interesting story, full of incident and adventure, with an admirable spirit attending it consonant with the kindly and sweet, though courageous and energetic temper of the distinguished philanthropist.—*American* (Philadelphia).

THINK AND THANK is a most useful corrective to race prejudice. It is also deep y interesting as a biographical sketch of a distinguished Englishman.—*Philadelphia Ledger*.

A fine book for boys of any class to read.—*Public Opinion* (Washington).

It will have especial interest for the boys of his race, but all schoolboys can well afford to read it and profit by it.—*Albany Evening Journal*.

Told simply and well.—*New York Sun*.

An excellent story for children.—*Indianapolis Journal*.

The old as well as the young may learn a lesson from it.—*Jewish Exponent*.

It is a thrilling story exceedingly well told.—*American Israelite*.

The book is written in a plain, simple style, and is well adapted for Sunday-school libraries.—*Jewish Spectator*.

It is one of the very few books in the English language which can be placed in the hands of a Jewish boy with the assurance of arousing and maintaining his interest.—*Hebrew Journal*.

Intended for the young, but may well be read by their elders.—*Detroit Free Press*.

Bright and attractive reading.—*Philadelphia Press*.

THINK AND THANK will please boys, and it will be found popular in Sunday-school libraries.—*New York Herald*.

The story is a beautiful one, and gives a clear insight into the circumstances, the training and the motives that gave impulse and energy to the life-work of the great philanthropist.—*Kansas City Times*.

We should be glad to know that this little book has a large circulation among Gentiles as well as among the "chosen people." It has no trace of religious bigotry about it, and its perusal cannot but serve to make Christian and Jew better known to each other.—*Philadelphia Telegraph*.

Bound in Cloth.   **Price, postpaid, 75c.**

HISTORY OF THE JEWS.

VOL. I.

From the Earliest Period to the Death of Simon the Maccabee.

BY PROFESSOR H. GRAETZ.

OPINIONS OF THE PRESS.

The style is distinctly popular, and it unquestionably represents the prominent features of the period with accuracy and spirit.—*Philadelphia Ledger.*

Aside from his value as a historian, he makes his pages charming by all the little side-lights and illustrations which only come at the beck of genius.—*Chicago Inter-Ocean.*

The writer, who is considered by far the greatest of Jewish historians, is the pioneer in his field of work—history without theology or polemics . . . His monumental work promises to be the standard by which all other Jewish histories are to be measured by Jews for many years to come.—*Baltimore American.*

This is a work that has commanded the highest encomiums of the press, Jewish and Gentile . . . It is written in a plain, clear, narrative style.—*New Orleans Picayune.*

There is much of living interest in the work, which displays a fair and impartial spirit.—*Minneapolis Tribune.*

The work is not only a history, but is a fascinating one that cannot fail to entertain as well as instruct the reader.—*San Francisco Call.*

It is a well written, ably translated and interesting version of the history of a wonderful people.—*Brooklyn Eagle.*

It is well that this reliable and complete history of the "peculiar people" should now be translated into English and presented in available form to the public by the Jewish Society.—*Burlington Hawkeye.*

Professor Graetz's History is universally accepted as a conscientious and reliable contribution to religious literature.—*Philadelphia Telegraph.*

Bound in Cloth.   **Price, postpaid, $3 per volume.**

The Persecution of the Jews in Russia.

WITH A MAP, SHOWING THE PALE OF JEWISH SETTLEMENT

Also, an Appendix, giving an Abridged Summary of Laws,
Special and Restrictive, relating to the Jews in
Russia, brought down to the year 1890.

OPINIONS OF THE PRESS.

The pamphlet is full of facts, and will inform people very fully in regard to the basis of the complaints made by Jews against Russia. We hope it will be very widely circulated.—*Public Opinion* (Washington).

The laws and regulations governing Jews in Russia, subjecting them to severe oppression, grievous restrictions and systematic persecution, are stated in condensed form with precise references, bespeaking exactness in complication and in presenting the case of these unfortunate people. —*Galveston News.*

This pamphlet supplies information that is much in demand, and which ought to be generally known in enlightened countries.—*Cincinnati Commercial Gazette.*

Considering the present agitation upon the subject it is a very timely publication.—*New Orleans Picayune.*

It is undoubtedly the most compact and thorough presentation of the Russo-Jewish question.—*American Israelite.*

Better adapted to the purpose of affording an adequate knowledge of the issues involved in, and the consequences of, the present great crisis in the affairs of the Jews of Russia, than reams of rhetoric.— *Hebrew Journal.*

Paper.   **Price, postpaid, 25c.**

RABBI AND PRIEST.
A STORY.
BY MILTON GOLDSMITH.

OPINIONS OF THE PRESS.

The author has attempted to depict faithfully the customs and practices of the Russian people and government in connection with the Jewish population of that country. The book is a strong and well written story. We read and suffer with the sufferers.—*Public Opinion* (Washington).

Although addressed to Jews, with an appeal to them to seek freedom and peace in America, it ought to be read by humane people of all races and religions. Mr. Goldsmith is a master of English, and his pure style is one of the real pleasures of the story.—*Philadelphia Bulletin.*

The book has the merit of being well written, is highly entertaining, and it cannot fail to prove of interest to all who may want to acquaint themselves in the matter of the condition of affairs that has recently been attracting universal attention.—*San Francisco Call.*

RABBI AND PRIEST has genuine worth, and is entitled to a rank among the foremost of its class.—*Minneapolis Tribune.*

The writer tells his story from the Jewish standpoint, and tells it well.—*St. Louis Republic.*

The descriptions of life in Russia are vivid and add greatly to the charm of the book.—*Buffalo Courier.*

A very thrilling story.—*Charleston (S. C.) News.*

Very like the horrid tales that come from unhappy Russia.—*New Orleans Picayune.*

The situations are dramatic ; the dialogue is spirited.—*Jewish Messenger.*

A history of passing events in an interesting form.—*Jewish Tidings.*

RABBI AND PRIEST will appeal to the sympathy of every reader in its touching simplicity and truthfulness.—*Jewish Spectator.*

Bound in Cloth.   **Price, Post-paid, $1.**

THE SPECIAL SERIES, of which "The Persecution of the Jews in Russia" is the initial number, is supplementary to the books issued by the Society, and will be supplied to all members of the Society without extra cost.

It will be published from time to time, and will be devoted to papers, original and selected, on topics of timely interest.

The issues will be uniform in style and shape, so that they can be preserved and bound in volumes.

———

ALL PUBLICATIONS FOR SALE BY THE TRADE AND AT THE SOCIETY'S OFFICE.

———

SPECIAL TERMS TO SCHOOLS AND LIBRARIES.

———

JEWISH PUBLICATION SOCIETY OF AMERICA,

OFFICE, 714 MARKET STREET.

PHILADELPHIA, PA.

www.ingramcontent.com/pod-product-compliance
Lightning Source LLC
Chambersburg PA
CBHW022014050726
47499CB00007BA/2584